The Door of the Unreal

by Gerald Bliss

Originally published in 1919.

I

THE BRIGHTON ROAD

My name is Lincoln Osgood, my age thirty, my nationality American, my means—well, such as never to cause me a moment's anxiety or the negation of any fad: my hobbies have always been travel and science, the latter more particularly in its human than in its mechanical aspects. I am not, if I may say so. in any way the "Yankee millionaire" of popular fiction or even of fact. I both write and talk the King's English, I trust; and to tell the truth, I was educated up at Christ Church. Oxford, which is my first link with these extraordinary incidents, which it has now fallen to my lot to chronicle.

It was up at Oxford ten years ago that I first met Burgess Clymping. with whom. from the first night we sat next to each other in the wonderful old hall of the House with its centuries of historical portraits. I struck up the great friendship of my life. He was a year younger than I, the owner of a nice property in Sussex and had seen but little of life in those days. whereas I had travelled a lot even then for my age. It is the accident of this long friendship and my travels in obscure and unfrequented parts that brought me into the circle of the strange doings I am about to relate—to which, by good luck. I held the key.

I am in no way the hero of the piece—if hero, in the conventional sense, there be at all—not even the protagonist, as the Greeks used to call it. I am merely the "handy man" of the play, so to speak, who chanced into the middle of this unconventional drama at its height, and helped to see it through ro a conclusion as strange as anything which has ever occurred in the whole annals of this country: and I have been asked by the other actors in this bizarre play in very real life to collate me facts and document them for themselves and such others as may be interested in these things beyond the door of the unreal, though, for reasons which will become obvious, they can hardly be released for general indiscriminate publication.

To the ordinary stay-at-home person of both sexes, who does not travel, eats eggs and bacon for breakfast every day. and does not realize a yard outside "Little England." they will seem merely absurd, the imaginings of an ill-balanced mind. Yet none the less they happened actually on and within a very few miles of the Brighton Road in the second decade of this modem age of motoring.

I am no expert at telling an extraordinary story and making it convincing; but I have an instinctive feeling that. in trying to do so. one has a better chance of carrying conviction by telling it as far as possible in the first person without too much underlining of the capital "I's" or seeking the limelight for oneself, filling up the inevitable gaps and interstices with actual documents and statements by such other immediate actors in the drama as can tell their part of the story firsthand. So. when this story ceases to be direct and straightforward, it will be documented, vouched for and, as far as possible, dated. This is my apology for obtruding myself—at the express desire of the others concerned in these extraordinary happenings.

DOCUMENT
From The Sussex Daily Times, February 4, 19—
THE MYSTERY OF THE BRIGHTON ROAD

During the early hours of yesterday morning, too late to be reported in our issue of yesterday, a two-seated car was discovered apparently abandoned nearly half-way up Handcross Hill. It was in the ditch on the left-hand side of the rond and had wedged itself securely. The tail-lamp and off-side lamps were still burning: but the engine had stopped. It was discovered by a Mr. Holmes. who was motoring back to London from Brighton. He stopped and called oul; but, getting no reply, he concluded that the occupants had run into the ditch and, being unable to get the car out again, had gone in search of help.

It was full moon and a very clear night: and, as there was no sign of anything wrong or anybody hurt. Mr. Holmes. being late, drove on. He stopped, however, at the police-station at Handcross and notified the officer in charge.

A constable was dispatched upon a bicycle, and returned in due course to report that apparently there was nothing wrong. He had found the rug lying a short distance from the car and had replaced it on the seat. He apparently saw no sign of anybody, though he had cooeed and blown his whistle several times. He went back to take charge, as the necessary lamps were burning and the car was on it's own side of the road, he apparently made himself as comfortable as possible with the rug wrapped round him, and dozed off and on in the car.

As soon as it grew light enough a breakdown party was dispatched, and the car was extricated from the ditch. It proved not to have been much damaged and was taken to the station, where the first sign of anything seriously wrong became evident.

On the cord upholstery of the seat there was a large stain of congealed blood frozen hard. This placed a totally different complexion upon the matter, and steps were immediately taken to inform the higher authorities.

The car. which was a 12-h.p. Rover, bore the identification number "B.P. 318726." showing that it was a local one. "B.P." being the identification letters for West Sussex: and in the course of the morning it was discovered to be the property of Mr. George Bolsover. a young gentleman farmer, of Heighbury Farm. near Crawley.

Inquiries elicited that he had gone out the evening before, about 5.80, in his car with his wife to spend the evening with a friend at Hassocks—Mr. Glentyre of Orchard Place. He had arrived at Orchard Place with Mrs. Bolsover shortly after six o'clock, and had played billiards with his host until dinner-time. Alter dinner Mr. and Mrs. Bolsover and Mr. and Mrs. Glentyre had played bridge until past upon midnight.

The Bolsovers had left in the highest of spirits in the car: and Mr. Glentyre himself had tucked the rug found by the car, which he identified, round Mrs. Bolsover. From that time up to going to press nothing has been seen or heard of either Mr. or Mrs. Bolsover. who appear to have vanished completely.

The whole country round is being scoured by the police: but the hard frost of the last ten days precludes any material assistance, such as footprints or similar traces, which would help to guide the police or give any clue as to what happened either before or after the car was ditched.

All railway stations and ports are being closely watched: and all reports of strangers are being immediately followed up.

So far there is not the slightest clue and the whole affair of the Brighton Road is wrapt in the deepest mystery.

Some strange scratches have been found upon the paint-work of the car, according to the latest message by telephone from our chief reporter, who has been on the spot all day.

The police, who are very reticent, have a theory, and anticipate shortly to be in a position to throw light upon the extraordinary disappearance of Mr. and Mrs. Bolsover, which is complicated by the bloodstain upon the upholstery of the car.

The case is in the eminently efficient hands of Chief Inspector Mutton.

II

DOCUMENT
MEMORANDUM BY LINCOLN OSGOOD

It would be hopeless to try to convey the sensation, the rumours, and the columns in the press with reference to '"the Mystery of the Brighton Road." which immediately captivated the imagination of the public. A volume of Hansard would not contain a tithe of what was written round the disappearance of the Bolsovers, the false reports, the theories, the letters to the papers from indignant public and assiduous amateur detectives alike, and so forth, the mystery gripped and fascinated the public as happens from time to time and there was a strange undercurrent of nervousness behind much of the indignation. It seemed so impossible that in well-administered, twentieth-century England a man and his wife could disappear without a trace out of their own car on the most motored road in the country.

Murder, highway robbery, kidnapping were all put forward, but nothing was discovered to justify in the least any of the theories. A deliberately planned and cleverly executed double disappearance was favoured by many, but there was the bloodstain to be accounted for. Again, there was no motive, no incentive for any such disappearance, the Bolsovers were a most devoted couple and had only been married a few months. They had no monetary troubles—in fact, were in '"affluent circumstances." as the reporters put it. They were leading the ideal life of their own choice in a nice old house, farming sufficiently without making a burden of it, hunting a couple of days a week, shooting, motoring into Brighton to shop, and generally putting in a good tune with plenty of friends.

There never was an affair so motiveless and therefore so sensational.

But. do what the authorities could, never a trace nor a clue turned up that led to anything or even afforded a shadow of a solution. Within a few weeks the sensation burnt itself out by its own intensity and died a natural death, and other happenings, in their turn, ousted this "Mystery of the Brighton Road" from a foremost place in the papers and the public mind.

At Scotland Yard it was duly collated and docketed: and the dossier was filed in the limbo of undiscovered crimes. Yet at the same time. apart from the ominous bloodstain, there was nothing tangible to point to the fact that it was actually a crime at all.

And that was the last of the poor devoted young Bolsovers—a dear little woman and a genial good fellow without an enemy in the world.

III

From Town Tit Bits, March 20, 19—.
QUERIES PERTINENT AND IMPERTINENT

. .. Whether the Upper Chamber and the Footlights are once more about to unite forces?

. . . Whether Wuffies and Tony are taking the situation as seriously as some other less interested folk?

. . . Whether Manager King of the "Castle" regards the latest Town Tit Bit as a good "ad" or a lost star?

IV

DOCUMENT

CONTRIBUTED BY WILLIAM WELLENGHAM, 2nd LIEUT., COLDSTREAM GUARDS

I never was much of a hand at writing, and am a bit nervous about trying to tell my portion of this weird story, but Lincoln Osgood says That I have got to. and that's all there is to it. It is up to either Harry Verjoyce or me. and Harry says he is worse at it even than I am: and Osgood has promised to put my statement shipshape. But he wants it told direct and in my own words, as I was on the spot throughout this particular bit of this incredible tale, which frankly I wouldn't believe myself if I hadn't been through it, and old Harry is ready ro swear to it as gospel.

My name is William Wellingham. commonly called "Bill." aged twenty-one, and a subaltern in the Coldstreain. So are Tony Bullingdon and Harry Verjoyce, and the same age as myself. We were in the same house at Eton, and pals from the very start, and we went on to Sandhurst together, and from there were all gazetted into the Coldstream. Tony is what they call in novelettes a "belted earl" and "the catch of the season," as he owns three big places and a substantial slab of London property, which he inherited from a whole line of rigidly pious ancestors, who never did anything to cause him a moment's anxiety by gambling or mortgaging as much as a single acre. Moreover, the whole lot had the additional advantage of accumulating for years "during the minority of the young Earl of Bullingdon," as the society papers said when he came of age last year, and we celebrated it by the big theatrical dance at the Savoy, which made all the uninvited people in London green with envy: but that is another story, as one of the minor prophets or minor poets once said. But it is really not altogether outside the radius of this statement of mine, as it was at his own coming-of-age dance that Tony first met poor old Wuffles, as Miss Yvette St. Clair. the leading lady in the "Castle" revue, was always called amongst her pals and the people who wanted to pretend to be smart.

It was a sort of what people call an infatuation on both sides—more on his than on hers perhaps: and there was no end of talk about it in town during the winter, and lots of people thought he was going to many her, and some of the impertinent rags began to get quite rottenly personal about it before the end. Tony is a good-looking chap—not too big. but very smart and full of life. So was Wuffles, who was as pretty as they make 'em, off as well as on, which you can't say for every girl on the stage, and a jolly good sort into the bargain, as straight as a die and no nonsense of that sort about her. That's what makes a lot of these theatrical marriages nowadays, and set inquisitive people guessing in this particular case, but that's none of my business. Poor Wuffles has gone—and it makes me sick to think of it—and poor old Tony almost went too, and now that he is fit and about again and there are other tidings in the air. I would not have referred to the matter. If it hadn't been what the lawyers call relevant. Anyhow, it was the talk of the town. and things were stoking up that Sunday, April 1 (this is no April fool yarn, I give you my word!) when we went on that fatal run to Brighton and ended up with a top-hole jolly dinner at the Royal York before returning to town by moonlight.

Tony was driving Wuffles in his 90-h.p. Napier, the one he used to race at Brooklands. and I always used to think she must have been jolly uncomfortable in it on the road, as it was hardly the most suitable machine for a girl: but it was his favourite, and she always pretended to like it. The rest of the party—that is. Harry and myself with Cissie

Saxon and Clemeuce Rayne, also of the "Castle"—were in Harry's new Daimler. a topper, the latest model just delivered, and. if we had to take his dust on the road. we were at any rate a jolly sight more comfortable. People may think, by the way, that I am a bit indiscreet in mentioning names, and so on: but. though it may seem a trifle off and a bit embarrassing, there are no two ways to it, and that little party, all said and done, has been well enough advertised in every quarter of the uncivilized world a hundred thousand times by now.

As I have said. we had a top-hole jolly dinner with plenty of "boy," though not enough to make any difference to the driving. Tony was always jolly particular when he was driving the big Napier, as she was a bit of a handful on the road. But we were all very merry and bright, and chipped Tony and Wuffles quite a lot about the paragraphs in Town Tit Bits; and there is no saying what it mightn't have led to, if it hadn't been for the ghastly sequel.

Closing-time came all too soon, but with one thing and another it was eleven o'clock before we were all tucked in and ready to start. I heard the clock strike as we waved and shouted good night to a few kindred souls, who had come out to see us off. It was a ripping night, cold and frosty and almost as clear as daylight in the fall moon. Harry, of course, was driving his own "bus with Clemence up in the front beside him; and Cissie and I were in the back, well wrapped up, and all as jolly as sand-boys.

There was a bit of a delay while Tony got his big engine going—a beast to start when it was cold; and we got off ahead of him, thinking how riled he would be if we reached town fast. But we hadn't got more than four or five miles out, when we heard him roaring up behind us: so we slowed down and drew to the side to let him pass. As they flashed by Wuffles waved her hand triumphantly, and shouted something we could not catch because of the noise of his engine with its open exhaust. That was the last ever seen of Wuffles, poor girl: and who is to say what might not have happened to us if Tony had been delayed a bit longer, and we had kept in front as far as Handcross Hill?

We slowed down almost to a walking pace for a mile or two to avoid their dust. just jogging along till it got a bit clear: and Cissie and I not unnaturally got talking about the extraordinary disappearance of the Bolsovers, as I suppose everyone else motoring on the Brighton Road had done for the past two months. We had both of us passed the spot a dozen times since the event; but somehow the place and the subject had a curious fascination of its own. And it was hardly surprising considering how full the papers had been of it: but that was nothing to what was to come. when they fairly got their glut of it.

After a bit the fog of dust began to clear, and we could see our way almost like day by the light of the full moon, so we began to put the pace on a bit not to get left too far behind. It was a topping night for speeding up, with a clear road, and Harry soon let the car right out, impatient after having had to hang about so long. The Daimler, though not a racing machine, was pretty fast too, and it did not seem long before we found ourselves beginning to climb Handcross Hill.

"Funny light ahead," called out Harry from the wheel.

"Looks like a fire." I shouted back. "'Hope it's not the old Napier!"

But sure enough it was: and there the tragedy began.

In a moment we were right up to it—not in the road or in the ditch, but blazing in a field the other side of the hedge within a few yards of the Bolsover business. It was for all the world as though something had gone wrong with the steering-gear, and it was not till later in the development of the story that we learnt the whole horrible truth.

"Good God." Harry ejaculated, putting on his brakes pretty hard and nearly taking a dry skid.

The girls began to scream, and I thought Cissie was going to faint, but I hadn't much time for that sort of truck just then, and was out of my side of the car almost before we had stopped. Harry was only a second after me, as he had to disentangle himself from the wheel and Clemence, who clutched hold of him in her fright and horror. There was a great gash torn in the hedge, through which we jumped, and on the other side in the ploughed field, which was frozen hard. lay what was left of the Napier—on its side blazing for all it was worth. It was obviously impossible to save the car or do anything to it, and we dashed forward to see if we could rescue Tony and Wuffles, or whether they had been thrown clear.

A glance showed that there was no sign of either of them in or under the car. The holocaust had not gone far enough to leave any doubt of that, although some of the wooden-headed police tried to insist first go off that they had been burnt but both Harry and I were firm on the point.

"Thank God." we both exclaimed at the thought that they had at least escaped such an awful death, and then we started to draw the ground round to see where they had been thrown. A few feet from the car I trod on Tony's cap; but, strange to say, there was no sign of them anywhere within reasonable radius.

They had both disappeared as totally and absolutely as the Bolsovers!

There was no lack of light between the moon and the blazing car; and there was no doubt about it.

"You take this side of the hedge," I called out to Harry, as I dashed back through the gap, "and I'll take the other."

The girls, white as death and sobbing hysterically, were hanging on to each other against the side of the car.

"No sign of either of them." I shouted, trying to buck them up. "At any rate they aren't burnt."

And no sign of them there was either. Harry and I drew the hedge on both sides, the road, the ditches, and again the field, making wider and wider detours, till we felt that it was pretty hopeless and made our way back to the blazing car, which was getting red-hot and beginning to buckle about the frame.

We looked into each other's faces. All he said was, "Good God, Bill"; and all I said was. "Good God, Harry"—both feeling that there was something deeper behind it, something intangible and uncanny, something beyond our crude ken. And we made our way slowly back to the girls, and in the minds of both of us was the memory of the Bolsover mystery.

As we got back to the old Daimler, we heard the sound of another car hooting as it came tearing up the hill: and Harry and I jumped our into the road and yelled to it to stop. The driver was already slowing down at the sight of the blaze on the other side of the hedge; and he turned out to be an awfully good chap—Fitzroy Manders by name, as I found out afterwards. He had a pal with him called Greville: and there were two ladies in the back of the car.

I explained to him as shortly as I could what had happened, though in rather disjointed fashion, I'm afraid: and I saw his face grow pretty grave in the white light.

"It looks devilish fishy," was all he remarked: and he went back to his own car and said a few words to the ladies. The one on the near side got out; and he beckoned me to join them and introduced me.

"My wife. Mr. Welliiigham." he said without any frills, as I raised my cap.

"My wife and her sister will look after the girls with you." he added. "Naturally they must be frightfully upset by this extraordinary business. They had better get into my car, and Greville will drive them up to Handcross and leave the ladies at the Red Lion: and then he can bring the police back with him."

He had a strong, managing way about him which was very welcome after the shock, which I don't mind admitting had knocked me out a bit—and old Harry, too—while the girls were a jolly sight worse, and on the verge of hysterics. Mrs. Manders proved a topper, and took Them in hand with a few kind words, and had them in her car before you could say knife, tucked in securely between her sister and herself to give them a nice sense of companionship and protection

Greville jumped into the driver's seat. while Manders cranked the engine.

"Drive like the devil." I overheard him say to Greville. "There is no saying what may not be out on this ill-omened hill to-night."

And off they went as though there were no hill at all.

"Now," said Mauders curtly, "draw your car well in on its own side; and then we'll have another search." There was little left by that time of the famous old racing Napier save red hot iron and distorted metal. So that did not delay us long, and under Manders' direction we started a methodical search, but all to no purpose, and not a trace of anything, except poor old Tony's cap, could we discover.

We found ourselves back on the road again and searched it up and down once more without the faintest result.

Manders lit a cigarette and passed us his case: and I noticed Harry's hand was a bit shaky, as though he had had a late night. So was mine. I don't mind confessing.

"There is something damned funny at work somewhere." said Manders, in a detached sort of way, as though he were thinking hard, "especially coming on top of the Bolsover case. Hullo! there's the car"—and we heard it hooting down the hill, hell for leather.

Two minutes later it was alongside us, and out jumped a sergeant and a couple of policemen almost before Greville had drawn up.

"I have telephoned Chief Inspector Mutton, sir," said the sergeant, saluting Manders, " and have left orders to advise Scotland Yard immediately, and I have telephoned to Crawley to send assistance by car without a moment's delay."

"Excellent." said Manders. and he explained the whole situation to the sergeant in as few words as possible: and I couldn't help marvelling at the clear concise way he put things. But then it turned out afterwards that he is a barrister, you see; so I could hardly be expected to compete.

"It looks on all fours with the Bolsover case," said the sergeant, when Manders had finished. "I had a good deal to do with that business myself, and know the ground pretty well. If you don't mind. sir. I think we had better have another search."

And after he had examined the car, which had nearly burnt itself out, he organized the seven of us, and we drew every inch methodically in an ever-widening circle.

Help was not long in arriving from Crawley. and in little over an hour Chief Inspector Mutton was on the spot and had taken over from Sergeant Handcock. And by daybreak the whole place was alive with all sorts of people.

Lincoln Osgood says that I can now hand over to him and retire, as I have shot my bolt, and I am jolly glad, as not only do I hate writing, but it is particularly hard to write about that awful night, which will always remain a nightmare in my mind.

V

DOCUMENT

CONTRIBUTED BY SIR HENRY VERJOYCE, PART., 2nd LIEUT., COLDSTREAM GUARDS

I am a worse hand even than Bill Wellingham at writing; and Lincoln Osgood says that there is no need for me to go ovcr thc ground again, as Bill has already covered fully the only part I could deal with first hand. So all I have got to do is to testify that every word of his statement is gospel truth: and to this I herewith append my signature for what it is worth by way of corroboration.

(Signed) HARRY NERJOYCE

MEMORANDUM
By LINCOLN OSGOOD

I do not enter the story of these strange events directly at this point, but I feel that a memorandum collated by myself will, at this juncture, save the publication of a burdensome number of documents from the press and other sources, and help to state my position concisely and put things in perspective.

This naïve, but convincing statement, contributed from direct participation and observation by young Wellingham, brings the evolution of this chronicle to a point infinitely more sensational than the disappearance of the comparatively obscure Bolsovers, and it is hard even to suggest the enormous and unparalleled excitement, not onlv in Great Britain. but all over the world. It may almost be said that even the more sober section of rhe press thoroughly let themselves go over it, while the "yellow" oracles fairly went mad over such a sensation as the disappearance of the richest and most eligible parti in the peerage and the most popular leading lady in revue, whose names had been coupled together by gossip under such romantic circumstances—especially under such inexplicable and extraordinary conditions following so close upon the heels of the Bolsover mystery. The very familiarity of the spot at which these tragedies had occurred added fuel to the flames of excitement: and. moreover, a new element of fear had entered the realms of commonplace everyday life and gripped the public imagination.

The sub-editors of the halfpenny papers ran riot over the new mystery of the Brighton Road, and "featured" it with headlines suggestive of some of the organs of my native country, and no wild or fatuous rumour was considered too impossible or foolish to find a place. The reporters made high holiday all over the country, especially between London and Brighton, and Sussex was obsessed day and night by "specials" and space-men in search of copy. Even the leader-writers, locked in their sanctums in Fleet Street, were busy evolving theories without availing anything.

But to revert to the point at which Wellingham's statement left off, all the searching of the police proved unavailing, and though they looked wise and hinted at clues in response to the importunities of the legion of pressmen. Chief Inspector Mutton and the cracks of the detective force from Scotland Yard had glumly to admit amoungst themselves that they had found not a single thing to help them. and did not see a single ray of light through the utter darkness any more than in the case of the Bolsovers, who had retreated right into the background as a minor and subsidiary issue in view of the later and far greater sensation.

It must be frankly admitted that everything was against them, especially the state of the ground, which was as hard as iron, and had been frozen on the night of April 1 and the early hours of the morning of April 2; and. to crown all, with daylight it had begun to rain, and settled down into a regular downpour as the day went on. This not only precluded the use of bloodhounds, which had actually been telephoned for, but soon reduced the ploughed land and the vicinity to a sludgy condition, which in a short time became pock-marked with the footprints of the many searchers to the exclusion of any possible traces which might have escaped observation.

Photographs of Lord Bullingdon and Miss Yvette St. Clair, already familiar enough to the pubic were circulated immediately throughout the country, and every port, station, and all other such possible places were closely watched. In fact. every member of the public might have been said to have constituted himself or herself into a private detective—all without the least result. Moreover, there was nor the slightest object in any such voluntary disappearance, especially when preceded by the dangerous feat of wrecking a fifteen-hundred-pound racing-car—less object in fact. I may say. than there could have been even in the case of the Bolsovers.

Town Tit Bits, in its usual impertinent way, hinted at an elopement engineered upon original lines, or at least, a big theatrical advertisement for Miss Yvette St. Chair of a fashion that left the imaginative efforts of any American press-agent cold stiff, and a million miles behind.

A certain section stuck to the theory that the bodies had been burnt in the holocaust of the car; but, apart from the direct and unshakable evidence of Wellingliam and Verjoyce, expert examination absolutely negatived the possibility. In fact, no one familiar with the history of the disposal of bodies by burning and the interesting cases on the subject in the annals of criminology gave it a moment's serious consideration in the circumstances. Besides, there was the Bolsover parallel, and their joint disappearance under circumstances identical, save for the wrecking and burning of the car, was directly against the theory of incineration.

The theory of motor bandits and the victims being held up for ransom was the most popular one of all, and had. on the face of it, more logic and possibility behind it, but here again rose the Bolsover parallel to question it. If ransom were the object and kidnapping the solution, why had two whole months passed without any word or attempt to reap the benefits of such a bold criminal stroke. Of course it was possible, dealing admittedly with a criminal gang of very exceptional ability and organization, that the victims might be held for a considerable time or until a sufficiently large "bag" had been accumulated, and. of course, if so, in Lord Bullingdon and Miss Yvette St. Clair they had indeed, consciously or unconsciously, dropped upon a haul as rich as any in Great Britain, which would, properly handled, assure such affluence as to render minor business in the future superfluous.

These are the in impressions on my own mind, when I landed in England after some months of travel through the remoter parts of Austria. Poland, and the Balkans on the evening of Monday, April 2. and read the first accounts of the whole business in the evening papers, which were full of it. And from that moment I never lost touch with the whole horrible, yet fascinating business until a tiny clue- a thing that would have meant nothing, save to one person in a million, which I had chanced upon in my travels- placed in my hands the key to the solution of this apparently inpenetrable mystery. I claim no great perspicacity or credit in the matter for myself -far from it. I see in it rather the hand of Providence bringing me with the specialized and requisite piece of recondite knowledge on the spot at the psycological moment, in time to prevent further similar tragedies and to prove instrumental in eradicating the foul curse which had fallen upon Sussex out of the mysterious realms of the real, yet the unreal at the same time.

I had promised Burgess Clymping that I would go straight down to stay with him as soon as I reached England, and what I read in the papers of the "Mystery of tlie Brighton Road" fascinated me, and made me all the more eager not to delay a moment more than absolutely necessary in making good my promise, as his place Clymping Manor, is less than three miles off the Brighton Road and the scene of the two remarkable dual disappearances. Crime and mystery have always held my interest closely, and I have studied the subject most carefully from the scientific, the analytic, the human, and every other point of view. In fact, I may say that even now there are few places in which I can spend a more interesting afternoon than the Chamber of Horrors (so called) at Madame Tussaud's. reconstructing the famous crimes of the past, and interviewing, in wax, the greater and lesser exponents of murder "as a fine art."

I was too late to go down to Clymping Manor that same night, and in addition. I had certain business to transact the next morning in London in view of my long absence abroad. So I wired to Burgess that I would be with him the next day by the 3.50. when I stepped, personally and directly, right into the thick of it. Meanwhile, he will fill the gap with a most interesting and sensational happening, which I just missed personally by this delay.

VI

DOCUMENT

CONTRIBUTED BY BURGESS CLYMPING, OF
CLYMPING MANOR, NEAR
HANDCROSS, IN THE COUNTY OF SUSSEX

I must frankly confess to having been obsessed from the
very first by the Bolsover affair on the Brighton Road, and
it is perhaps only natural, as it happened so near to the
boundaries of my own estate, but I never dreamt what a
part I should find myself called upon to play in the
elucidation and clearing up of the whole ghastly affair.

Within three miles of my own home, and less than half
the distance from the family, Dower House, lay the scene
of the two mysterious disappearances which had convulsed
the whole country: and, great as had been the sensation
over the Bolsover business, it was child's play compared
with that which followed the affair of Tony Bullingdon and
Miss Yvette St. Chair.

I had naturally worked with the police and rendered what
personal assistance I could in the former case, all to no
result. The local part of the business had proved itself
utterly hopeless and entirely barren of any clue long before
the police 'would admit it even with the utmost reservation
to the public. If the earth had opened and swallowed the
Bolsovers. like Korah, Datlian. and Abiram. their
disappearance could not have been more complete.

My name is Burgess Clymping: and Lincoln Osgood, my
dearest and closest friend, who at the immediate request of
myself and all the others concerned, has consented to act as
chronicler and collator of the events surrounding and
explaining this extraordinary mystery, certainly the
strangest of modern times in its dénouement and all that lay

behind it, has in my opinion, in his preliminary covering memorandum, said sufficient about me personally for the purposes of this record,

I live at Clymping Manor, which has been in the possession of my family in direct and unbroken succession since the fourteenth century, and I have often felt it my duty to marry as the last of the line for this reason alone, but hitherto I have never had any real inclination—or rather the real inclination. I am not particularly wealthy, but the estate, which runs to some six thousand acres, renders me very comfortable and well-to-do as country squires go, and affords excellent shooting, which is my particular hobby. I farm nearly a thousand acres of it myself in a rather practical way; and that keeps me pretty busy, and my time fairly occupied.

My constant companion is my only sister, Ann, a beautiful girl of just upon twenty-one, who keeps house for me and looks after my guests and myself in a most delightfully capable, yet unobtrusive fashion: and it is this, perhaps, which has kept me from ever contemplating marriage seriously, save as an abstract or academic duty to the House of Clymping. Our mother died when Ann was a child of three and I a boy of thirteen, and my father five years later, so it will easily be understood that she has meant very much to me all her life and has always been my special care.

Now that she is grown up and. as I have already said, is a very lovely girl—tall, active, and wonderfully fair, a rare thing in these days, with remarkable grey eyes with long black lashes and arched black brow, and a magnificent lithe figure (I could write lots about Ann's beauty and good points as but this is hardly the place to let myself go) feel that it will not be long before love claims and then, perhaps, marriage will assume a different personal perspective in my eyes. This, at any rate, is how I felt on

Monday, April 2, but much has happened since then which will come out in the evolution of this story; and I must frankly admit that certain vague ideas had already been chasing themselves tlirough my mind more or less inconsequently without taking any very definite shape. But I am wandering from my brief and anticipating unduly.

Clymping Manor is a commodious, if unpretentious, early Georgian house of mellow red brick and large windows, panelled throughout, and above everything comfortable. The head of the family had in 1742 deserted the original old manor house, a small but perfect piece of Elizabethan architecture, which lay buried in a hollow a mile and a half away. and built a more spacious and healthy family mansion upon the highest point of the estate, with terraced gardens sloping down to the woods, and there is no question that he did well by subsequent generations of Clympings, the old manor house has since been used as the Dower House, as it is now generally called but, there having been no family claimant to its use since the death of my grandmother four years ago, it is let at present to an eminent German scientist, Professor Lycurgus Wolff, who took an extraordinary fancy to it last summer when he struck it by chance—trespassing, I may say. with all a foreigner's disregard of our insular sanctities—upon an entomological expedition, whilst staying in Brighton.

I did not like the idea of letting it. I must frankly admit: and it was not the rent that attracted me so much as the fact that it had been standing empty, apart from the occupation of the kitchen quarters by one of the under-keepers and his wife as caretakers, for close on four years, and was getting into a somewhat damp and musty condition, as it must be admitted it is a bit dank down in the hollow amongst the trees. However, as there appeared no likelihood of it being required again for family purposes for many years to come, and as the Professor was importunate and produced unimpeachable references, in the end I consented to let it to him furnished for a year. It was a bit of a wrench sentimentally, as from a boy I have always been particularly attached to this beautiful little Tudor manor in miniature, a perfect gem in its way from an architectural point of view, as the old home of the Clymping family—the actual original house on its site having disappeared centuries before, save for part of an old stone barn attached to the Dower House.

Thus it came to pass that Professor Wolff took up his residence in the Dower House last autumn. He was a very striking-looking man of sixty, with shaggy grey hair and beard, a pair of remarkably piercing black eyes under long, straight, slanting brows, which met in a point over his nose, and distinctly pointed ears set low and far back on his head, half-hidden by his long hair. His mouth under his straggling, unkempt mustache was full and red-lipped, and he had a very fine set of even, white teeth, especially considering his age. His hands were long and pointed, projecting curiously far at the third finger, and noticeably hairy, with red almond- shaped, curving nails. He was tall and rather lean, with a slight stoop, and walked with a peculiar long swinging stride—altogether a strange and rather bizarre personality in the surroundings of sleepy Sussex, especially as in winter he always wore a Russian cap of grey fur and a heavy grey fur coat.

However, he proved an interesting and intellectual companion, widely travelled and widely read; and though I did not see very much of him, from time to time we interchanged visits and met by chance about the place. Three times during the winter he and his daughter dined with us.

He lived a very simple sort of life with his books, his writing, and his collection of strange insects, alone save for his daughter, Dorothy, and one middle-aged serving woman. Anna Bruunolf by name, a rather sinister person with grey glinting eyes who had been Dorothy's nurse and was, whatever her appearance, obviously an industrious and capable servant. Dorothy—well, it is difficult to give my first impressions of her, except that she was as unlike the Professor as anyone could well be, and without the least trace of the Teutonic type but that is another tale, and again I must not let my pen outrun my story.

Suffice to say, she struck me as beautiful—beautiful in a way totally different from my Ann, but possessing a rare beauty that grows on one—her hair, brown and waving, with a strong red light in it, and a wonderfully clear complexion, small delicate features and two great solemn blue eyes that looked on life as though they had not fathomed it; considerably shorter than Ann, but beautifully built, a fact that her rather rough-and-ready clothes could not altogether conceal, and the daintiest hands and feet I ever saw on any woman. The matter of first impressions is always difficult, especially when the question of dress enters into them: and Ann, in due course, helped to change or, at least, to modify that to the revelation of a beauty of form, which was hidden under the dowdiness of garments dictated by an elderly German professor, absorbed in other things, and a distinctly autocratic nurse of the type of Anna Bnmnolf, who had no taste in such matters, and had been accustomed more or less to rule Dorothy almost from the cradle in the persistent fashion it is hard for a girl to shake off even at two-and-twenty.

A great friendship sprang up between Ann and Dorothy almost from the first, though neither the Professor nor Anna seemed to encourage any particular intimacy; and the result was that Dorothy was far more in our house off and on than Ann, who could not bear the Professor, ever was at the Dower House, with the distinctly repellent personality of Anna Bruimolf, in a funny brown fur cape which she habitually wore, ever appearing dour and uncompromising at the massive oaken front door studded with old nails— one of the original and most picturesque features of the old Tudor house—which was habitually kept shut instead of open in English country-house fashion. No one else in the neighbourhood took the trouble to cultivate my new tenants particularly; nor were they encouraged to do so, the Professor giving it to be understood that he was deeply immersed in a great work on entomology, the magnum opus of his scientific career, which was to make his name famous not only throughout the world, but to posterity for all time.

On reading over what I have written I am afraid that I have, after all, let my pen run away with me in these preliminaries; but, as a matter of fact, I really ask no pardon, as they are all more or less relevant to the story in hand, and will help those interested to grasp more clearly local surroundings and those connected with and instrumental in unravelling the mystery, which, for a while, looked like proving a blind alley. Nevertheless, it is high time that I got back to Monday, April 2, the point in the action of the story from which I am detailed to start my personal contribution.

I was awakened that morning at a quarter to seven by Jevons, my faithful butler and valet, who had practically grown up with me on the estate, and in many ways was almost a foster-brother; and I saw at once from his pale, scared face that there was something wrong.

"What's up. Jevons?" I asked before he could speak, sitting up in bed.

"More trouble on the Brighton Road, sir," he answered; speaking with suppressed excitement. "Another couple have disappeared out of their motor and vanished—just like the Bolsovers. Hedges has just been up from the lodge, as he thought you would wish to be informed as soon as possible."

Quite right," I replied, jumping straight out of bed. "Tell him to wait, and put out my old shooting-suit. I'll have my bath when I get back. Don't tell Miss Ann until she is dressed, and ask her not to wait breakfast. Make me a sandwich while Wilson brings round me two-seater."

I was hardly five minutes slipping on my clothes and ate my precautionary breakfast in the car, as we hurried along, with Hedges (who is my head-keeper) on the dicky-seat behind.

It was a beastly raw morning; and a cold, uncompromising drizzle had set in, which turned into heavy persistent rain, as the morning went on, removing any possible traces which might have been left to aid the police.

We were soon on the spot and found it fairly alive with police summoned from all parts, including detectives from Scotland Yard, who had arrived by car. There was also already quite a gathering of local sightseers standing open-mouthed, and several reporters had got wind of things and turned up by car or bicycle; but the police had formed a cordon round the immediate vicinity to keep everyone back. However, recognizing me, they let the car pass; and I approached a little group standing round Chief Inspector Mutton.

He saluted me and told me everything in a few words, adding in a low voice, for my private benefit, "It's an exact repetition of the Bolsover lousiness, except for the burning of the car, sir, and looks equally hopeless."

Then he introduced me to Fitzroy Manders, whom I knew by name as a rising barrister who had been up at Balliol two or three year's before my time; and he in turn introduced me to Verjoyce and Bellingham, who between them told me their story firsthand and save me details of the fruitless searching which had already taken place. Then we strolled across to the car, which was nothing but a charred and twisted heap of scrap-iron.

"This rain puts the lid on it," said Manders, with a slight shiver; and I noticed that he and the two younger men looked white and starved with cold.

"You had better come up to my place with me and get a hot bath and some breakfast, if Mutton doesn't think we can do any good," I said, learning that Greville had gone to Handcross an hour before to drive the women-folk back to London,

They readily assented, and I sent them on ahead in the Daimler with Wilson and a message to Ann, while I returned to Mutton, who was arranging for a fresh search with the C.I.D. man from Scotland Yard.

I placed Hedges and Reece, the underkeeper, at their disposal, and threw myself into it heart and soul; but at the end of an hour and a half we forgathered again with nothing to report. It was raining hard by then; so I left them for a while and drove myself back in the two-seater to the house, where I found the three others bathed and breakfasted, and looking little the worse for their night out, though the two youngsters had a curious strained look on their faces.

Ann was busy entertaining them and had heard the whole weird story in every detail; and it spoke well for her nerve that she had not turned a hair.

"What news?" they all asked at once.

I shook my head.

"None," I answered. "It looks pretty hopeless, especially with the rain setting in heavily for the day. We'll go back after I have changed and breakfasted."

I went up to my dressing-room, leaving them to smoke, and got off my wet clothes, bathed and shaved, and was soon down again, eating a hearty breakfast with a real country appetite which no sensations could put off.

Soon after eleven we drove back to the spot again and spent a fruitless morning in the soaking rain. A large crowd had collected, and was kept back with the utmost difficulty by the reinforced police; and there seemed to be importunate reporters at every turn—but no news.

Mutton was disgruntled and rather morose.

"It's a bad job," he said disconsolately, "and we shall have the whole press and the country In its wake down upon the incompetence of the police force. Major Blenkinsopp from the Yard is down—he's the second-in-command at headquarters—and he frankly does not see what more can be done."

I was introduced to Major Blenkinsopp and had a short talk with him; for which I was glad; as it put me into direct touch with him, which proved immensely useful later on; as will be seen; but he would not come back with us to lunch, as he was anxious to get back to town.

So we returned to the house shortly after one and were back again soon after two, only to find things just as they were, and the rain falling more heavily than ever.

At four o'clock, realizing the futility of hanging about any longer, Manders and the two youngsters decided to return to town in the Daimler; and I went back home a little later, leaving instructions for word to be sent to me if anything turned up unexpectedly. But of this there seemed little hope.

I was thoroughly tired by the excitement of the day and the long hanging about, which I often think takes more out of one than any amount of honest exercise and really doing something; and so was Ann. But we were both mightily cheered up in the middle of dinner by a telegram from Lincoln Osgood to say that he had arrived in London and would he with us the following afternoon. No news could have been more welcome at any time, but it was more than ever so at such a juncture, when I felt the need of a friend to talk things over with, and I knew what a profound interest he would take in the extraordinary mystery, though I did not then imagine that it would be he who would hold the key to it, and put his finger with bold, unerring instinct upon the unthinkable clue which was baffling the cleverest detective brains in the whole country.

After dinner I smoked a large, soothing cigar in front of the blazing wood fire in the hall, glad to be cosy and indoors with the outside elements shut out; and naturally we talked over the strange events of the day and the mysterious fate of Tony Bullingdon and Miss Yvette St. Chair, whom we had seen in the revue at the "Castle" only a month previously, little dreaming what the morrow was going to bring forth to link us both up so much more closely with the weird affair.

"Anyhow the Brighton Road will be well patrolled to-night," I said, as I kissed Ann good night soon after ten, when we both felt quite ready for bed; and, sensation or no sensation, I must confess to having dropped off to sleep almost at once and slept soundly all night.

I was up again at six the next morning thoroughly refreshed, and was on the spot again by seven, after an early breakfast. Fortunately, it was a lovely morning, bright and warm, with the sun shining and it seemed to infuse a spirit of optimism, which had been sadly damped by the weather and lack of success the day before, into Inspector Mutton and his now considerable army of policemen and officials, both in uniform and in plain clothes.

Nothing, I learnt, had transpired in the night; and we were doomed to another futile morning which led to nothing, kicking our heels and reading the sensational articles in the London and Brighton papers, which ran to columns in each, mainly imaginative journalese culminating in the trite assurance that the police had the matter well in hand, but were not in a position at the moment to issue any statement.

Fed up with doing nothing, I returned to the house about noon for an early lunch, hungry after my six-thirty breakfast and long morning in the open air. When I had finished I tried to settle down, but somehow I could not; and something seemed to draw me back to the spot irresistibly. So, whistling to my wire-haired terrier, Whiskers, who is ever my constant companion in my perambulations round the estate, I decided to walk down through the woods, putting a flask and plenty of tobacco in my pockets, mindful of the discomforts of the previous afternoon, and leaving orders for Wilson to pick me up with the car in good time to meet Lincoln Osgood at Crawley.

Ann volunteered to accompany me part of the way; and I was only too delighted to have her company. We walked through the gardens, examining the progress of the bulbs as we went, and let ourselves out into the park by the little gate at the comer, striking across diagonally to the left through the woods,

About half-way, where they are thickest, under half a mile to the left of the Dower House, Ann suddenly stopped.

"I don't think I will come any farther with you, dear," she said. "I don't want to get amongst the crowd or go to the place itself."

I agreed with her thoroughly, and nodded my approval.

"I think I'll go across to the Dower House and fetch Dorothy back to spend the afternoon with me, It won't be so lonely with you away."

"Quite a good idea," I assented heartily. "I'll take you across to the bridle-path and go that way. It's not much out of my way."

Somehow I had a dislike of the idea of leaving her there alone in the thickest of the wood with the mystery of such strange things hanging over our heads and tragedy in the very ah" so we took a half-turn to the right with me instinct bom of familiarity with our own woods, in which a stranger, once off the path, would have run a risk of losing himself irretrievably and wandering in a circle.

Whiskers was trotting to heel according to habit; but about a hundred yards further on he stopped suddenly and began to whimper excitedly, his ears pricked and his right paw off the ground—a way he had got if anything unusual interested him.

"What's wrong, old chap?" I asked, stopping and turning round to him.

He made as though to cast to the left and ran a few steps, and then halted, whimpering again, "Good dog," I said, little thinking of what was about to happen. "Find it."

Off he darted, and ten yards away he stopped and looked back at me as though wanting me to follow.

Then he began to dig furiously.

Ann, full of curiosity, was after him instantly; and I was not far behind.

And there we found Tony Bullingdon! He was practically hidden from sight in a short, deep gully between two big trees, half covered with last year's leaves, which the winds of the winter had swirled and collected into this small hole, little bigger than himself, into which he had fallen. What between the dead leaves, dank with rain, and the colour of his great motor coat, he was practically invisible a few feet away, and that is, I suppose, how it had happened that he had been overlooked in the search, which had, of course, been very difficult in the thickest part of the woods.

He was lying on his right side, and only the left portion of his face was visible, white and bloodless, and his left aim lay unnaturally limp, half behind him. His coat was torn on the shoulder, which was badly lacerated, with the blood congealed. His forehead, too, was badly cut, and upon closer examination he appeared to have been roughly handled or dragged along the ground and abandoned, but it was impossible to say how much was due to having been thrown from the car, though, as has often been proved, the steering-wheel, which had unmistakably marked his chest, had probably broken the fall. His heavy coat, which had also probably protected him considerably, was all torn and filthy, and he proved to be a mass of bruises from head to foot when we got him home.

Ann gave a little involuntaly scream; and Whiskers continued digging at the leaves furiously until I called him off.

I bent down and examined him. He was icy cold and absolutely unconscious, but his heart was beating faintly; and I thanked God that I had slipped my flask into my pocket. I tried to raise him gently and forced a little whiskey between his clenched teeth; but he moaned painfully, and I realized that his collar-bone was broken, if not his whole shoulder-blade shattered. However, I managed to get my arm underneath to lift him a little. Then I ran my hands gently over him, opening his motor-coat, and found to my satisfaction that, owing to the leather lining; he was not so saturated underneath as one would have expected.

"Bar his lefl-shoulder and collar-bone, I don't think there is anything broken, though I am not sure of a couple of ribs on his right side, as I daren't turn him over alone," I said to Ann, who was standing by, pale but self-possessed. "His right ankle is badly sprained, too. I can't move him by myself in case I do any damage."

"I'll wait here while you go for help," she said calmly; and, nervous and unhappy as I felt at the idea of leaving her alone, I saw at once that there was no other way out of it.

"The nearest policeman keeping people off is only just over half a mile away," I said, assenting. "I won't be more than a few minutes. I'll send him on to Mutton for a bearer-party and the doctor, and come straight back to you. Rub his hands gently with some whisky from my flask," I added, loosening the laces of his brogues and pouring some spirit into them as I spoke. "I will leave Whiskers to guard you."

Then, without another word I made off, as fast as the trees permitted, in the direction of the bridle-path.

I found the man without difficulty and dispatched him hotfoot to Inspector Mutton; and it was not much more than a quarter of an hour before I was back again.

To my surprise I found that Ann was not alone, and recognized through the trees, as I drew near, the strange figure of the Professor in his grey fur cap and coat.

Ann was seated on the ground with young Bullingdon's head in her lap; and the Professor was busy doing his best to bind up the shoulder and collar-bone with strips of what I recognized as Ann's petticoat. His large sharp pocketknife lay on the ground; and he had cut off the clothing in the way, and was working skilfully and deftly with his curious long fingers, which had always fascinated me.

"The poor young man!" he exclaimed, looking up for an instant, as I approached. "I was taking a ramble through your woods—"

(" Trespassing as usual," I could not help but thinking, a trifle grimly)

—'when I heard your dog bark and then growl; so I came in this direction, and it was all Miss Clymping could do to keep him quiet."

Frankly I did not care a damn about his explanation, as I saw he knew his job and was the right man in the right place at the moment.

"His collar-bone is broken, and the shoulder has been put out and possibly broken," he went on, as he worked; "but it is so swollen that I can hardly tell. Two right ribs fractured." Then he began endeavouring gently to restore the circulation. "Give him some more whisky out of your flask." Then he slipped off his fur coat and wrapped it round the poor unconscious, white-faced boy, for which I could have blessed him.

"Miss Ann had better go back to the house, and get a bed aired and ready and a big fire lit," he continued, speaking as one accustomed to give orders; "and you can roll your jacket up and make a pillow for his head in place of her lap,"

"Yes," I said, speaking for the first time, as I helped Ann up, shifting his head as little as possible. "Run home, Ann dear, and get everything ready. Telephone to Handcross and Crawley for doctors immediately, and send Jevons and Wilson and anyone else handy along as fast as possible with brandy, blankets, pillows, and the big luggage barrow with a mattress on it; and don't forget my first-aid case."

Ann was as pale as the lad on The ground, but quite calm, as I pressed her arm encouragingly.

"I won't be long," was all she said, as she started off in her quick, athletic way; and I knew instinctively that everything would he ready.

It will be touch-and-go," said the Professor, not stopping in his work; as he talked, "especially if pneumonia supervenes; but he is young, and the exposure was not so great as it might have been owing to his heavy leather-lined coat. His head is a bit bruised, but the cut on the forehead is not as serious as it looks."

I could not but feel grateful to him for his psychological appearance and all that he was doing; and I thanked him perhaps a little inconsequently.

He only shrugged his shoulders.

'It is lucky my afternoon walk took me this way," he said as calmly as though it were an everyday occurrence. "The police called at the Dower House on their search yesterday; and that was the first I had heard of this extraordinary event. Of course I could not help them at all; but this afternoon I thought I would go down to the scene of the accident, or whatever it was, and see if they had found anything. Yes, it was fortunate. Chafe his left foot, please."

He spoke perfect English, but with a strong guttural accent; and I obeyed him instinctively, feeling that he knew what he was about. It was less than half an hour before Inspector Mutton arrived with four policemen and a couple of C.I.D. men; and I told them exactly what had happened, explaining also the lucky accident of be Professor's presence.

Mutton was obviously in a state of suppressed excitement, but distinctly disgruntled that the discovery had not been made by the police; and he said very little. He stooped down and picked up the pieces of Bullingdon's motor-coat, Jacket, and underclothes, which the Professor had cut to bits with his sharp knife in slitting them off the body.

"You say the cloth was all torn and lacerated, sir?" he asked, turning to me.

I nodded.

"They will afford us precious little clue now," he said ungraciously, as he examined them. "They have all been hacked to pieces; and no one could draw any deductions from them in the state they are."

"It was necessary," intervened the Professor sharply, showing his white teeth a little angrily. "There are occasions when you cannot wait for the police, when you are doing their work."

It was put rather brutally, and Mutton took the rebuke with obvious bad grace and turned on his heel busying himself with orders to his men and a consultation with the detectives from Scotland Yard in an undertone; and I felt that, if ever he could do the Professor a bad turn and get his own back for the snub in front of his own men and the more important representatives from London, it would be done with his whole heart.

It was nearly an tour after Ann had left us that I heard Jevons calling through the wood, and the waiting seemed interminable; and after that it was frightfully slow and difficult work carrying Bullingdon through the close trees to the luggage-barrow. Several times the poor chap groaned; but the Professor; who; unasked, had undertaken the direction of operations to the chagrin of Mutton, took little notice.

"A good sign," was all he said.

At last we got him as comfortable as possible on the barrow; and, hearing from Jevons that the doctors were on their way, the Professor turned to me and bade me good afternoon without taking the slightest notice of anyone else.

"Then I can be of no further service." he said as coolly as though he were leaving a tea-party; "so there is no need for me to accompany you, I will resume my fur coat, if I may, as the patient is now wrapped in blankets, and I am rather susceptible to chills. I only trust that I have not got one myself."

I helped him on with his treasured coat and thanked him again, not. however, without a certain reaction at his apparent callousness and readiness to shift further responsibility, but I really had no particular desire for his presence at the house, with my own doctors available.

He waved his hand to me. turned on his heel, and swung off with his peculiar long stride as our little cavalcade started on its slow and weary progress.

It took what seemed an interminable time to get back to the house in our endeavour not to shake or jolt Bullingdon more than was unfortunately unavoidable; and, when we got there, we had to get him upstairs—fortunately a wide staircase—and into bed.

Everything was ready, and two doctors waiting and Ann instinctively fell into the role of head nurse, for which she was well fitted not only by nature, but by a course of "first-aid" which she had insisted upon after leaving school.

So it was a quarter past five before I found my self down in the hall again; and, as I rang for Jevons to bring me a large whiskey and soda, I remembered for the first time that I had forgotten all about Lincoln Osgood and meeting his train.

MEMORANDUM
By Lincoln Osgood (continued)
qzAzqt this point I enter the action of this strange narrative directly, and henceforth the writing of it will be quite straightforward and falls altogether, or practically altogether, to my pen. The preceding documents have gathered together first-hand all the threads of the story, which I was loth in the peculiar circumstances to deal with second-hand, as when this manuscript is complete, each of the extraordinary happenings will then stand vouched for by eye-witnesses and direct participators, leaving no room for doubt or allegations of imagination, such as is part and parcel of mere fiction.

Now to the story, as I entered it at 4.30 P.M. on Tuesday, April 3, upon my arrival at Crawley Station.

I must admit that I was surprised not to find the car waiting to meet me, as it was so unlike methodical and hospitable old Burgess, who had never once before failed to be on the platform in person.

Naturally I was disappointed not to see his familiar form, but I guessed there must be some good reason. After waiting about expectantly for a quarter of an hour I cast round for a conveyance, but found considerable difficulty in finding one, as, what between police, reporters, and morbid sightseers, everything seemed to have been engaged.

At last, just as I had made up my mind to foot the seven miles to Clymping Manor, I managed to commandeer at an extortionate price a ramshackle old fly, which drove up and deposited a load of excited visitors from Brighton, full of the latest gossip.

"There's a rumour that they've found some-thing in the Clymping Woods," one of them volunteered in his self-importance; "but nobody knows what yet."

"It may only be another rumour." interjected one of the others pessimistically.

So this was the reason of Burgess's absence, I thought to myself: and I bade my bottle-nosed old charioteer make his overworked horse put the best of its four doubtful lees foremost.

"This gentleman's for Clymping Manor," the porter vouchsafed, claiming importance in his turn, and I immediately became the cynosure of all eyes—a figure of mystery, the latest importation from Scotland Yard. an unofficial Sherlock Holmes or what not!

I sat back in the rickety old conveyance and lit a cigar, making myself as comfortable as possible in view of my prospective hour and more of jolting: and it was no small relief when, a little over halfway, a car approached at something considerably over the futile English speed-limit and drew up with a scrunch, the chauffeur calling out something to my driver.

I put my head out and recognized Wilson; and it was not long before I had transferred myself and my baggage to the car, much to the relief of my charioteer, who pocketed his ample fare at the saving of half his long double journey.

In the car Wilson told me what had happened, explaining fully how it was that Burgess had overlooked the time and could not come himself, and I was naturally all agog to get to the house.

At the entrance of the drive I found a constable on duty, who let us pass at once on recognizing the car; and there was another policeman at the front door—a strange sort of reception.

Burgess was out on the step before the car had stopped, and wrung my hand between his.

"Forgive me. old chap." he began

"It's all right," I answered, interrupting: "I quite understand. Wilson explained to me as we came along. But are you sure I shan't be in the way?"

"Quite the reverse," he replied, with decided emphasis, as he led the way in. "I have never looked forward to your arrival more or waited a pal so badly—or Ann either. You are the one man I can really talk to; and God knows I badly want someone to whom I can unburden myself,"

He helped me off with my heavy coat with his own hands: and I felt it was good to be welcomed so warmly.

Then we went into the old panelled hall, which I had always thought just the jolliest place in the world and looked upon as the real embodiment of home on my distant travels.

"It is good to be home, old man." I said. warming myself in front of the big log fire as he poured me out a drink, which I needed badly after my journey. "Somehow, as a roving bachelor, I always look upon Clymping Manor as home, and make for it the moment I arrive in England."

"That's good hearing. You know we have found young Bullingdon?"

I nodded.

"Yes; and I hope it's the first step towards unravelling this extraordinary mystery It struck me right in the face when I landed yesterday; and nobody seems able to talk about anything else."

"It was all new to me, but I've lost no time in reading it up: and you must tell me all about it. How is Lord Bullingdon?"

Burgess shook his head.

"Devilish bad: but he is young and strong. The doctors are with him now; and I have telephoned to town for Sir Humphrey Bedell who, by luck, turns out to have attended his family for years. He is bringing down Sir Bryan O'Callaghan in case an operation is needed, and a couple of nurses. At present Ann is in charge. We shan't get much chance of a yarn to-night, I fear, between doctors, nurses, and detectives."

And so it turned out. It seemed one long procession, all one after another, coming to Burgess for this thing and that. First one was Inspector Mutton and the C.I.D. men, who announced that Major Blenkinsopp was on his way; and then the local doctors, looking very grave and rather important.

They confirmed what Professor Wolff had said, but agreed that he had done very well with the limited means to hand. They had set the fractures and dressed the wounds, and incidentally spoke very warmly of Ann's help. Of the shock and concussion they could say very little; and they could not directly account for the torn shoulder, which had looked very angry, but appeared to be settling down wonderfully.

"As to the question of exposure, he would probably not have lasted though another night, and it was really only his greatcoat that saved him as it is," said Dr. Drake: "and I hope that with his youth and constitution we may stave off pneumonia. With any luck he may pull through; but it is impossible to say anything much at present."

At Burgess's suggestion the doctors agreed to stay on until the specialists arrived from London; and he went off to see the housekeeper about dinner at some indefinite hour for the four doctors, Major Blenkinsopp, and anyone else who might turn up. So, despite the quiet that prevailed, it was a very busy house, every few minutes one or other of the doctors going up to have a look at the unconscious patient; but I did not catch even a glimpse of Ann, who would not leave the room for an instant.

It was not long, either, before Major Blenkinsopp arrived on a fast car which had wasted no time; and later he told us, with a cynical laugh, that he had been twice held up by the police on the way down for exceeding the legal limit. I was very glad to meet him; and he proved a most interesting, capable man, of great coolness and sound judgment, tall and soldierly in appearance, with a lithe, active figure, somewhere approaching fifty, with a rather sallow skin suggestive of India, and a grizzled moustache.

After hearing the doctors' report he went up to the sick-room for a few minutes in order to identify Lord Bullingdon, whom he happened to know slightly personally and very well by sight—the first actual personal identification—just to make certain that there could be no mistake.

Then he took Burgess off to the library, which had been handed over to the police as headquarters, and. after carefully going into his personal story, he interviewed Inspector Mutton and the Scotland Yard men, and heard all that they had to report.

A little over an hour later the London doctors arrived, with two nurses in a second car; and, after a few words with the local doctors, they all went up to the sick-room.

Watching it there in the hall, and occasionally entering into a bit here and there, it seemed to me for all the world like a scene upon the stage out of a well-mounted melodrama, but I had to possess my soul in patience so far as Burgess was concerned, as I did not like to ask questions of anyone else, feeling the anomaly of my own position.

"What about his relatives?" I asked Burgess, during an interval.

"Curiously enough he has very few near relatives," he answered. "I spoke to Sir Humphrey upon the subject over the telephone, and he told me that he would get into touch with Colonel Gorleston, his uncle and until recently his guardian- who also happens incidentally to be his heir. He turns out to be in Ireland on the Curragh with his regiment- the 10th Lancers: and Sir Humphrey has telegraphed to him. It may be a day or two before he is over, if he happens to be at Gorleston Castle, which is right out in the wilds and does not get letters or papers till two days late. It looks as though he is; or the news yesterday would have brought him over by the first boat. But we shall see."

Blenkinsopp joined us; and over a drink we discussed the case while we waited for the doctors.

"By the way." I asked, "what about this man Manders, whom you speak of? Is he Fitzroy Manders- the barrister?

"Yes, that's the man," answered Burgess, "a very interesting and clever chap—at least, that's how he struck me. Do you know him?"

"Yes. funnily enough. I do. though not as a conventional London acquaintance. We ran up against each other in Rumania last year in an out-of-the-way corner and knocked about together for nearly a week. I promised to look him up in the Temple some time when I got back, and intend to do so. This will lend an additional interest to our meeting."

"Fitzroy Manders," said Blenkinsopp, "is rapidly coming right to the top and will go far. He is, as probably you discovered, a very keen criminologist and we often see him unofficially at the Yard. He is a man I have a great liking and respect for."

"So have I," I said. "It is funny that chance should have butted him right into the middle of this business. Had he any kind of theory?"

"No, no more than any of the rest of us, to be quite candid," answered Blenkinsopp, shrugging his shoulders a bit impatiently; "and even this finding of young Bullingdon promises so far to throw precious little light upon it as far as I can see. It looks as though Scotland Yard, which the public always expect to be omniscient and infallible, will come in for a lot of the usual criticism and find itself in very bad odour—unless, of course, some Sherlock Holmes is sent from Heaven to expose our follies and futilities, and unravel amiably the whole mystery in that peculiar lucid fashion that always suggests that the story was written backwards. Our end is the brick-wall one, and a damned thick one, too, in this case, so far as one can judge."

"The more unusual and bizarre a crime." I ventured, "the easier it is of solution, as a rule, but here, so far as I can judge, unusual and bizarre enough, as it is in all conscience, no thing yet seems to stand out that gives even the most subtle imagination a pointer to build from. Hallo, here are the doctors."

The four doctors came down the wide oak staircase, speaking in low tones; and I noticed the old Chippendale grandfather clock struck nine as they reached the bottom.

We all three rose from our seats, standing expectantly and waiting for Sir Humphrey Bedell to speak.

"We can't say very much at present," he said in his quiet, well-modulated voice, born of forty years of sick-rooms and death-beds. "Sir Bryan O'Callaghan and I have been over Lord Bullingdon most carefully, and Sir Bryan has done a couple of very minor operations, but otherwise Dr. Drake and Dr. Forbes had done everything that could be possible. Now all we can do is to wait upon events and see how he goes on. He is badly knocked about, but he has, to my personal knowledge, a splendid constitution, and was in the very best of health; and this should give him every chance. The one thing that puzzles us is the wounded shoulder and the lacerations through his clothes, thick as they were. Owing to that fact they are not, however, very deep or necessarily serious, but their origin is obscure. They look as though they had been done by some instrument with a double set of teeth. He could not by any chance have been worried by some dog or other animal, whilst he lay unconscious, could he?"

Burgess shook his head.

"Most improbable." he answered. "If so, the dog would probably have been found there or attracted someone to the spot, or gone on with the job. There was no trace or sign of any such thing, though that does not go for much under the circumstances and weather conditions."

"That German professor." interjected Blenkinsopp rather acridly, "seems, in his eagerness to get at Lord Bullingdon's injuries, to have destroyed any chance of a clue from the clothes by hacking them off the shoulder in small pieces with a sharp knife. Otherwise we might have had something to go on."

The doctor from town nodded; and Burgess made Major Blenkinsopp known to them.

"It is unfortunate, of course," said Sir Bryan O'Callighan, "but he did it for the best. In fact, I hardly see how he could have done otherwise."

"Well, anyhow. I shall go down to interview him in the moming," said Blenkinsopp, "and see if he can help in any way or put forward any suggestions."

"I have arranged. Mr. Clymping." went on Sir-Humphrey, "with your kind permission, for Dr. Drake to spend the night on the spot, and Dr. Forbes will relieve him in the morning. There is nothing that either Sir Bryan or I can do immediately by staying on ourselves, and we must

both get back to town later on. Dr. Drake and Dr. Forbes
have agreed to work it so that one or other is on the spot for
the present, and I will run down again to-morrow
immediately after I have got through my morning's work,
and. of course. I am always available by telephone, and will
return at a moment's notice if anything urgent should arise.
That, however, there is no reason to anticipate."

Burgess nodded.

"You and Sir Bryan will stay and have some dinner?"he
asked.

"Thank you." answered Sir Humphrey, "we shall be very
glad to do so; and then we can have another look at Lord
Bullingdon before we go."

Burgess left us once more to give his orders about dinner,
and then went upstairs to see Ann who sent down a
message begging to be excused, as she was having
something to eat upstairs with the nurses. Burgess told me
privately that she was bearing up marvellously, but was
very tired; and he had advised her to go to bed.

Blenkinsopp, who had accepted Burgess's invitation to
stay the night, had in the meantime put a call through to
Scotland Yard, giving them the latest report, and
announcing his intention to remain on the spot till the next
afternoon at any rate.

Then followed dinner at half-past nine. a strange meal in
its unexpected assortment of guests— the four doctors and
Blenkinsopp, with Burgess at the head and myself at the
foot of the table. We were all old campaigners with level
heads and good appetites which it took a great deal to
upset; and despite the exciting events of the afternoon and
the lateness of the hour, we all managed to do full justice to
the excellent dinner, which, in the face of difficulties, Mrs.
Morrison. Ann's excellent housekeeper, had arranged for
us.

Conversation was general and by consent in front of the servants we avoided the obvious topic which was uppermost in the mind of each one of us: and I can recall that it was very interesting and touched upon a variety of subjects, which I should have liked to have followed up farther, had circumstances permitted.

Over the port Burgess, half at my suggestion, half at Sir Humphrey's, gave us an admirable first-hand synopsis of the whole business from the disappearance of the Bolsovers; and Blenkinsopp added certain facts and criticisms, which placed us all directly in touch with everything. To me it was invaluable, on account of its preciseness and lucidity, in helping me to collate the whole story and all the persons of the drama, great and small, in my mind in proper perspective: and it served as a sound basis for subsequent deductions.

Soon after eleven, however, the doctors adjourned once more to the sick-chamber, and came down again a few minutes later with nothing fresh to report beyond the fact that all was quiet and apparently going on as well as possible. So we armed them with long cigars and packed them into their car and dispatched them to town. Sir Humphrey promising to be down about three the next afternoon.

Shortly after, Dr. Forbes left; and the four of us sat round the fire for a final smoke before going to bed. The talk was very interesting, turning principally upon crime, especially mysteries undiscovered and those supposed by the public to have been undiscovered because unrevealed in the papers. So I got no chance of any private personal talk with Burgess.

At one o'clock, after a final report on Lord Bullingdon's condition, we all went off to bed pretty well tired out. Burgess showed us each to our rooms, myself last of all.

"I won't stop for a yarn to-night, old man." he said, turning on the light. "I'm dead fagged; and we should probably sit up till cock-crow. In the morning I'll take you all over the ground and show you everything first-hand."

So we just said good night, and like an old traveler, I was asleep as soon as I was between the sheets, glad to be "home "again.

(Continued)

The next morning broke fine and warm, the best type of spring morning with a real promise of summer in it, a complete contrast to the hard frost of the early part of the year, which had apparently broken up with the heavy rain of Monday.

My room was next to Burgess's: and he arrived in his dressing-gown as Jevons brought my tea at half-past seven- and planted himself on the end of my bed, lighting a cigarette.

"No news to count." he said. as I sat up and stretched comfortably after a splendid night. "Bullingdon's had a quiet night—still comatose, but doing as well as expected. Drake appears satisfied, and the nurses seem to think everything is going as well as possible 'considering,' as they say. Blenkinsopp is dressed and is closeted officially with Mutton and the C.I.D.'s in the library. So you and I had better get bathed and dressed, as they will all be wanting breakfast, and then I will take you round. Ann seems wonderfully well, despite the shock and strain of yesterday, and is looking forward eagerly to seeing you."

"Not so much as I am to seeing her." I said. jumping out of bed. thinking of my special little girl pal of the last dozen years, who had grown up into such a beautiful woman. "So off to your bath, and I'll follow when I've shaved."

Half an hour later I was downstairs and found Ann
waiting on the terrace, looking a trifle pale, but very
delightful in white serge. She knew I liked to see women in
white, and I think she put it on specially to greet both the
promise of summer and her old friend.

She came forward with both hands outstretched. "Oh.
Line," she said, "it is good to see you again. You'll forgive
me for not coining down last night: but I wasn't up to it,
especially facing all those strange men at dinner after all
that had happened."

"Quite so," I agreed taking her hands and looking into her
face, "I thoroughly understood, poor old girl. But am I
getting too old to be kissed—or is it you?"

"Don't be silly," she said, putting up her lips and giving
me a frank sisterly hug with no nonsense in it.

"That's more like old times." I said- laughing. "By Jove.
Ann, you seem to have grown every time I see you—quite
a large-size, serious young lady instead of my tomboy in
short frocks."

"The gnawing tooth of time, Line, old dear. Why, I swear
you're beginning to get bald like all good young Americans
who roll in dollars. Hallo, here's Burgess to chaperon the
grown-up young lady, and keep her from saying pert things
to his respected guests."

And then, as we three strolled up and down the terrace,
she told me about her patient, as she instinctively dubbed
Tony Bullingdon, with quite a proprietorial air.

"It is awful. Line," she said. squeezing my arm. "to see
the poor boy—he's so nice-looking, too—there white and
unconscious, all bandaged up, and giving just an occasional
little groan or a moan—don't really know which you would
call it. He is awfully battered about by—well, whatever
happened, and I honestly thought he would die in my arms
with his head in my lap, while the Professor was cutting
away his clothes and doing what he could to bind him up—

with my petticoat, too, of all the funny things! He seems very clever, Professor; and I never saw such long, funny pointed fingers, but so quick and capable. He is so strange, too, when he is at work, so engrossed and abrupt, not saying a word except to rap out orders to me as though I were a lay figure; and I could not help being fascinated with his peculiar habit, which I had noticed once or twice before, of moistening—almost licking his lips with his long pointed red tongue. It seemed almost automatic as he worked, and was certainly unconscious. It made me feel a little sick— I don't know why—but he is certainly awfully neat and clever with his hands, and knows a lot about surgery and first aid."

"So all the four doctors cordially agreed," I said, watching her eager face, as we let her babble on, obviously relieving herself of much that had been pent up under the strain of necessity the night before. "But Major Blenkinsopp won't forgive him for having sliced up the clothes round the shoulder past all recognition or hope of clue."

"Oh, well, he really had to. They were all congealed and stuck into the wound in places," rejoined Ann, with a shudder. "Don't let us talk of it."

"No, poor old kid," said Burgess, bending and kissing her in the peculiarly nice affectionate way he has towards her, which has often made me think that one day he will make some lucky woman a particularly delightful husband. "I see Blenkinsopp and Drake kicking their heels: so let's go in and find out if breakfast is ready."

Blenkinsopp had nothing to report of interest, except that they told him on the 'phone from Scotland Yard that the papers, great and small, serious and sensational, had one and all spread themselves more than ever, and had run positively wild over the discovery of Lord Bullingdon, hinting at great disclosures impending.

"And so much the worse for us if we disappoint them," he concluded grimly; "and God knows it looks rather like as though we shall!"

Dr. Drake had nothing to add to Burgess's first report of his patient's condition: and before breakfast was over Dr. Forbes arrived to relieve him. So, after having seen Bullingdon together, Drake telephoned through to town to Sir Humphrey Bedell that all was well, and he confirmed his promise to be down round about three o'clock. Then Drake left; and for half an hour we scanned the bundle of daily papers, which Forbes had thoughtfully brought with him. In the normal way they are not due at Clymping till later in the forenoon: but Burgess gave orders for Wilson, for the time being, to fetch them each evening and first thing in the morning on his motor bicycle.

"Nothing but gas and journalese," exclaimed Blenkinsopp disgustedly, throwing down the last of them. "Later on, after I have seen Mutton again. I'll go down and interview this professor of yours at the Dower House and see if he can help with any idea or suggestion."

"I'll give you a note to him," volunteered Burgess. "He is a queer misanthropic sort of creature and resents intrusion, so it may make him more easy of access and inclined to be helpful—if he can be. I'll hang it on the peg of thanking him for what he did yesterday, and giving him news of the patient."

So they left me smoking and thinking idly. The word "misanthropic" had started a train of thought in my mind, illogical and indefensible; but I allowed my imagination to toy with it, as one often will, till Ann returned from the kitchen-quarters and claimed my attention.

"Men are such a nuisance to feed," she said. sitting on the arm of the chair next to mine "they do eat such a lot. Yesterday was a great and unexpected raid upon the larder, and this morning, in consequence. Mrs. Morrison and I have to restock and plan in advance for few or many without any clear knowledge of how many there are likely to be. I wonder if Lord Bullingdon's uncle, Colonel Gorleston, will turn up? Thank goodness he is a bachelor, under the circumstances! I should hate to have to entertain an anxious aunt-by-marriage of Lord Bullingdon, twice my age and more. and full of a sense other own great importance."

"You know you would do it very nicely. Ann, my child." I remarked banteringly "You have all the makings of a great and most expert hostess, in that you give people exactly what they like and don't worry them too much. But I, too, must confess to a feeling of relief, as it would make everything so infernally formal, and put us all upon our best 'boiled-shirt' behaviour. We shall probably hear about the gallant colonel, as people still term them in these perfectly peaceable days, from Sir Humphrey when he arrives after lunch. Hallo- here's the 'phone."

Jevons appeared from nowhere, as usual, and answered it. "It's Mr. Wellingham and Sir Henry Verjoyce, miss," he announced to Ann. "They want to know if they can come down."

So Burgess had to be fetched: and he told them they could come to lunch, though it was doubtful whether they could see Tony.

Then he was ready; and we set off with Blenkinsopp through the grounds, taking the way Burgess had taken with Ann the afternoon before, which, as he said, seemed weeks ago. We struck through the wood; and we found the place where the body had been discovered, roped off and covered with tarpaulins—not that there is much to preserve in the way of clues," as Blenkinsopp remarked cynically; "but Mutton is nothing if not thorough his desperation."

Then we put him on the bridle-path for the Dower House, and made across to the left to the scene of the disappearances. Burgess took me all over the ground minutely, up and down the road and in and out of the fields: but I must frankly admit it conveyed or suggested nothing fresh to me, interesting only as the actual spot of these strange happenings. The remains of the big Napier, which had been most carefully searched through without revealing anything of importance, lay in a heap where it had burnt itself out. also covered with a tarpaulin,

There was a greater crowd than ever, kept back by a cordon of police; and several reporters, who had been refused by Jevons at the door the night before and again in the morning, tried to fasten on to Burgess, whom they did not find very communicative, though the next day we found that they had managed to spin him out to a whole imaginative column and a half, much to his disgust.

"I'm getting fed up, Line," he said, calling me by the old familiar abbreviation, almost a nickname, coined, in fact, to response to my having christened him "Burge" in what he had termed my Yankee fashion; and "Line" and "Burge" it had always been between ourselves throughout the twelve years of our friendship. "Let's get off home; and be dammed to the lot of them."

But at that moment Blenkinsopp put in an appearance; and he asked us to wait a few minutes for him while he saw Mutton and the C.I.D.'s, got the latest reports, and gave some orders.

"All right. Mutton." we heard him say, as he rejoined us, "I'll leave after Sir Humphrey Bedell has seen Lord Bullingdon; so be up to report not later than three o'clock. Nothing fresh either here or from town," he added, as he reached us; "and it looks like a blind alley, the whole thing. Everything we do or try to do simply turns out to be wasted energy apparently, as so often the case in these matters. You would not believe how many men we have working upon the case all over the county.

Then, as he walked back through the woods, he told us about his interview with the Professor. At first he had been disinclined to see him, saying that he was tired of being interrupted by the police when he could do nothing to help them. Then he seemed to think better of it after reading Burgess's letter, and eventually was quite affable to him over a pernicious German cigar, which Blenkinsopp, who has a very particular taste in tobacco, had felt himself bound to smoke for diplomatic reasons.

"A very remarkable-looking man and a most unusual type," he said, describing him so vividly that I registered a little mental note I must meet him personally, "and undoubtedly very clever and well-read. He was more prepared to be expansive upon entomology and botany, his two hobbies, than to talk about the business in hand; but by judicially taking an interest in his bugs and plants, and smoking hard at his horrible cabbagio. I led him gently round, and in the end he answered all my questions promptly and lucidly, showing a well-ordered, logical brain. He described the finding of Miss Clymping and Lord Bullingdon and all he had done in the way of first aid. detailing the injuries as though entering up a case-book. He professed himself at a loss to account for the torn shoulder; knew of no dog locally likely to have found the body and tried to drag it to safety; certainly did not keep one, or for the matter any animals, himself— disliked them, in fact; had been forced to cut away the garments in small pieces from the wounded shoulder- as any other doctor would have done. He added that he had treated the wound with a wonderful ointment he always earned for use in case of bites or stings or other wounds— "not one you will find in your renowned B.P., as you call it," he had added, with a laugh, but he would guarantee that there would be no blood-poisoning now, whatever the cause of the wounds. He was affable enough, but seemed quite glad when I rose to go. and showed me out himself, so I fear there is not much to be learnt in that quarter—one more blind alley. He is evidently a very clever man." he concluded, "but frankly I did not cotton on to him somehow. There was something indefinable about him that repelled me—perhaps the insular Briton's dislike of that type of foreign savant outside his own particular circles."

However, what he had said about Professor Wolff had caught my cosmopolitan imagination; and I determined to meet this interesting, if not attractive, personality quite apart from the case in hand, whrch was obsessing us all so completely for the moment.

"But what a delightful little Tudor place you have got down there hidden in that damp hollow, Mr. Clymping," continued Blenkinsopp, "a regular architecuiral gem and a most paradoxical setting for our friend, the Herr Professor! That great studded oak door alone is worth going a good way to see, though I was not much impressed with the dour female with the brown fur tippet, who opened it to me."

And Burgess, drawn on one of his pet hobbies, held forth enthusiastically upon the beauties and history of the Dower House till we got back to the old Georgian mansion, which, with its greater size superiority of position, had supplanted it everywhere except in the atavism of its owner's heart.

We found that Verjoyce and Wellingham had just arrived; and after lunch, when Ann left us, Burgess and Blenkinsopp told them about the finding of Tony Bullingdon in filll detail.

"But what about Wuffles?" asked Bill Wellingham. "Tony would never have left her."

Blenkinsopp shook his head.

"Not a sign or a clue of the remotest description. She has, as far as can be ascertained, vanished as completely as the Bolsovers."

And for a few minutes we all smoked in silence without looking at each other. Soon after half-past two Dr. Drake arrived, and a minute or two after three Sir Humphrey's car drove up; and the doctors all went up together to see Lord Bullingdon.

There was no variation in their report, which was satisfactory so far as it went, especially as regarded the tears on the shoulder, which were doing very well: and Blenkinsopp told Sir Humphrey about the Professor's ointment, and he was obviously interested.

"But why was this not mentioned to Sir Bryan and myself last night?" he asked in his most professional manner, raising his eyebrows and turning to the other doctors.

"Because it was not then known to any of us," answered Burgess, intervening; "that is the reason why, Professor Wolff did not mention the matter either to my sister or myself; and she did not notice him put on any ointment. It may have been done when she was taking off her petticoat."

"Well, anyhow, the wounds are making wonderfully satisfactory progress," admitted the big man from London, apparently disinclined to probe the matter more deeply under such satisfactory conditions, which could only react favourably upon himself and his colleagues. "Colonel Gorleston has wired from Gorleston Castle that he will cross tonight; and I expect he will be down with you to-morrow night, but I will telephone you. I shall probably drive him down myself,"

As Lord Bullingdon was still unconscious, he allowed Wellingham and Verjoyce to peep into the room for a moment, and then left, offering Blenkinsopp a lift up to town to his car, which was gladly accepted.

The two youngsters left a little later, giving me my first quiet time with Burgess and Ann.

The next evening Sir- Humphrey arrived, bringing down Colonel Gorleston. who stopped till the following afternoon, when, feeling that he could do no good by staying on, he left with Sir Humphrey.

Meanwhile Lord Bullingdon continued comatose, but otherwise there was no change, but towards Friday evening he began to grow feverish and restless, and the next morning he was delirious, a phase which lasted several days, causing the doctors and all of us the greatest anxiety. All the time it was touch-and-go, and several times it seemed as though the thin flame of life had burnt itself out.

And his delirium was as strange as the rest of the strange case. He was continuously crying out "Wuffles," not in tones of love so much as those of horror, repeating over and over again the strange disconnected words; "Big dog ... jumped over moon... green eyes... big dog ... jumped over moon... green eyes.

It was his incessant cry day and right when not lying still in a stupor of exhaustion, The words were so ridiculous and bizarre in themselves, part and parcel of the bizarre character of me whole thing, that I must confess that in their very nonsense, reminiscent of the old nursery rhyme, they fascinated me and echoed through and through my head by the hour, to the exclusion of everything else, as I sat and smoked and pondered, trying occasionally to read, but without success. At times he babbled less boisterously of things having no possible connexion with or bearing upon the case, and then with redoubled excitement and horror he would take up the old cry of "Wuffles," followed by the same insistent words: "Big dog... jumped over moon ... green eyes."

It was a very absorbed and concentrated house within, with the shadow of tragedy and death hanging over it, doctors and relatives and police officials coming and going all the time, and from outside neither Blenkinsopp nor

Mutton had any developments or hopeful clues to report. They were frankly in despair and very down in the mouth: and everything looked hopeless.

On Monday afternoon, when Burgess and I returned from a walk, taken in the interests of exercise rather than anything else, we were surprised—and I was delighted—to hear that the Professor and his daughter had called to inquire after the invalid, and were at tea in the drawing-room with Ann. awaiting our return. I had intended to make Burgess take me down to call at the first opportunity; but one thing and another had prevented me from urging the point.

The daughter, Dorothy—a lovely girl, as Burgess has already described her in his "Document"—was dressed in white ermine with a cap of the same fur, which set off her beauty remarkably well—still in her winter things, perhaps not unwisely, as it had set in cold again on Sunday with the treacherousness of spring in England. She bowed rather shyly to me, when introduced, but the Professor held out his hairy hand with its long pointed fingers and almond-shaped nails, and. as I took it, a queer feeling of repulsion, both psychological and physical, came over me—a strange, unaccountable aversion to the touch.

Him, too, Burgess has described in detail, with strange slanting eye-brows that met over eyebrows, and his piercing black eyes. his low-set pointed ears. and his his red-lipped mouth with its conspicuous white teeth; and above all. I noticed, with a strange sensation, his peculiar swinging gait as he crossed the room towards me. He was apparently in his most affable and approachable mood, and deprecated any assistance he had been able to give.

"Ah, my magic ointment!" he said. with a guttural laugh. "The medical profession would give their noses to learn the secret of my famous concoction of herbs; but I will not divulge it, though I am no patent medicine-monger with a desire to make a large fortune by advertising it. Moreover, the ingredients are rare and unobtainable in this highly civilized county."

And he licked his lips with his long facile red tongue in the way already described to me; and I found that I could not take my eyes off the man. He fascinated me and set all sorts of strange, weird ideas coursing through my usually cool and well-controlled brain.

He made his inquiries into Bullingdon's condition, and appeared only passingly into the strange cry of his delirium, turning the subject with a shrug of his sloping shoulders.

"I am not a psycho-analyst," he said. turning to me, "I am absorbed in entomology and botany, and am writing a great master-work at present. Hence my presence in your quiet Sussex away from the many calls and distractions which surround me in my beloved Fatherland."

"I must admit to being fascinated myself, as an amateur, with this new science of psychoanalysis," I answered, dying to size him up and draw him out. "But I think of all subjects botany is the one to which I have given the most consistent attention in my travels."

I had struck the right note; and soon we were traversing Europe together—the Black Forest, the Austrian Tyrol. Poland, the Balkans. and the whole of the Near East. of which he showed an intimate first-hand knowledge. All the time we talked I watched him with a curious fascination which grew upon me every moment; and I was intensely disappointed when suddenly he rose quite abruptly to take his departure.

Burgess accompanied Miss Wolff to the door, and I. following with her father, could not help noticing his manner towards her, something indefinable and, perhaps, more an instinct on my part than anything else; but that, too, gave me much food for thought during the succeeding weeks. Had Burgess, hitherto apparently impervious, succumbed at last?

I helped the Professor into his grey fur coat. which I had already learnt was a characteristic of his appearance; and, as he put on his Russian cap of the same fur, he looked a most unexpected and strange figure in the old panelled Georgian hall.

"May I come down with Mr. Clymping one afternoon and see some of your specimens, Professor?" I asked, boldly forcing the invitation which had not been offered.

"I do not,,," he began: and then he seemed reconsider the question, "By all means, if they will interest you, as I fancy they will. So few people know anything outside the commonplace in these matters; but you seem to do so. It is so rare to meet a widely travelled man in this self-satisfied island."

And with these strange uncouth words, not too graciously spoken with a strong guttural accent, he turned on his heel without even the formality of shaking hands, preceding his daughter.

She turned and held out her hand, which I noticed was particularly small and dainty—quite unlike her father's, except as to the pointing of the fingers. ``"My father, like so many other geniuses," she said apologetically, "is very absorbed and absentminded."

She spoke in a soft well-modulated voice, free from accent: and for the first time I became fully aware of her charm. I had been so unpleasantly fascinated with the father that I had not had a moment up till then to pay any attention to the daughter, and I felt a guilty twinge at my unintentional rudeness: but, at the same time, I registered a mental vow to follow up his ungracious consent to my visit.

One thing and another had set up a wild train of thought in my head, and my brain was pounding hard like a big engine, as I sat smoking in the old hall after Ann had gone to bed; and Burgess, with the affinity of old friendship, seemed to realize it as he settled himself down to read the evening papers without comment.

At the end of half an hour I got up and helped myself to a drink.

"I am sony. Burge. old man." I said: "but I must run up to town to-morrow."

"Why?" he asked, looking up, with obvious disappointment in his voice.

"An idea has been working in my brain which I cannot discuss," I answered frankly. "It contains the germ of a theory too bizarre to put into words: and please do not press me upon the subject. I want to consult someone in town." I added "and Manders will do—if he be willing to take on the job I want. He is the very man to help. and I will approach him first; but not a word to Ann or Blenkinsopp or any living soul. I don't want to make an egregious ass of myself by flying too high, or too wide of human probability. I must probe and if possible, test my wild idea first."

"Why not me?" asked Burgess in rather a hurt tone.

"Because, my dear old chap in the first place are absolutely essential in Sussex; and, secondly, you might be out of your depth elsewhere."

Burgess nodded his characteristic nod of understanding.

"Will you take the car?

"No, thanks, I'll go by train, as I shall probably have to stay at least one night." I replied.

"But you will return? Promise me. God knows I should be lost without you at present, I grudge you even one night's absence."

"I will return." I answered, giving him my hand," whatever happens. I promise you to see this matter through to the bitter end."

And God knows, when I spoke those words by no means lightly, I never dreamt how bitter the end was destined to be.

BETWEEN LONDON AND CLYMPING

The next morning I went up to town by the 9.45 from Crawley: and Burgess drove me to the station, very loth To let me go. I could see, however, that he was both piqued and puzzled that I had not spoken more openly to him as to what was working in my mind: but the whole idea was so bizarre and at such an embryonic stage, that I frankly did not feel myself justified in unburdening myself at the expense of burdening him with what could only be throughout my absence an ever-present horror in his mind, as ghastly in its uncertainty almost as in its actuality,. if correct. Moreover, it was something entirely outside the scope of his mental diathesis, and would seem To him an utterly wild absurdity in the absence of any proof. Therefore I had decided, after turning the matter over in my mind from every point of view, that Fitzroy Manders was the only man to whom I could talk openly—the only man whose help I could enlist in the first instance at such an early stage of The ultimate possibilities.

In the Train I skimmed through all the morning papers, which were still full of The sensation, padding out the lack of anything fresh with a whole carnival of rumour, which may have served to appease the hungry public, but certainly took The matter no further from a practical point of view. Amongst them were one or two hot and windy attacks upon Scotland Yard and its ineptitude, which secretly rather pleased me, as They promised to make The difficult task I saw ahead of me easier at the psychological moment, when I should find myself forced to call in: official help in what was likely to be a very unofficial and certainly unconventional manner.

From Victoria I took The Underground to The Temple, making my way in by The Embankment entrance by the Library. Fitzroy Manders had chambers in the new buildings in Garden Court overlooking the beautiful old gardens; but in the train I had been struck with unpleasant misgivings as To finding him, as I had suddenly realized that it was the vacation.

And time was an urgent factor.

However, I was in luck, as his clerk told me that he had just arrived, being detained in town correcting the proofs of his new book on "Criminal Law," which he had not had time to finish while the Courts were sitting.

He ordered me to be shown in at once and welcomed me warmly.

"Osgood, by Jove, this is a pleasant surprise," was his greeting, as he shook hands cordially. "Wherever have you sprung from in your wanderings to and fro up and down die earth?"

"Clymping Manor;" I replied; and he started with surprise.

"By Jove," he exclaimed again, "of all the peculiar coincidences! How did that happen?"

I told him of my old friendship with Burgess, and the tie that always drew me there first upon arriving in England.

"And a strange state of affairs you found there," be commented. "Of course Clymping mentioned my name in connexion with the Bullingdon affair; and that is what recalled my existence so promptly to your mind?"

"Not exactly that," I answered, taking the armchair by the fire, to which he pointed. "I was intending anyhow to renew our very pleasant acquaintanceship at an early date; but it is on account of this strange mystery that I have run up to consult you to-day, much to the disgruntlement of poor old Burgess, and I hope to enlist your help."

"Anything I can do, of course." he said warmly. "But how? Have a cigar?"

He passed The box; and I took one and lit it without haste, pondering the best line of approach, while he seated himself upon the leather fender, puffing at his pipe.

"We are up against a very tough proposition, Manders." I began, and he nodded acquiescence— "up against the toughest thing you ever dreamt of in all the annals of crime: and I honestly believe that you are the only man in England—certainly the only man I can lay hands on—who can help me."

Manders shrugged his shoulders slightly in deprecation.

"They are at the end of their tether at the Yard, anyhow," he said, "and at their wits' end how to carry the matter an inch farther. I saw Blenkinsopp only yesterday and he admitted in confidence, which he won't mind my divulging to you, that it is a proper brick wall of a problem."

"Did he mention the German professor to you?" I asked.

"Yes: and he interested me very much as a type. What has he got to do with it?"

I liked his directness as a quick thinker.

"Possibly everything," I replied, "if my instinct be not playing a trick on me. I have a theory, strange and bizarre beyond all words in this humdrum twentieth century; one which touches a subject we discussed at considerable length one night in Rumania: and he is the key-stone, the pivot of the whole thing, which only came home to me as the result of my years of travel in the remote parts of the Near East. It is fantastic to a degree and may prove futile; and it is certainly not the sort of thing I would care To spring unsubstantiated upon cold-blooded officialdom for fear of being locked up in one of your polite lunatic asylums for the rest of my life. But I must have help—immediate help; and that is where you come in, if you will give up a month, or possibly less. of your valuable time. Time is of the utmost urgency to forestall the possibility of even worse happenings."

"It's the vacation fortunately," he said, "and apart from the last few pages of those proofs"— waving his hand in the direction of the big table in the window overlooking the gardens—"I have nothing to do but golf according to programme. So come along and unburden yourself fully to me. I certainly shall not think you mad," he concluded, with a little laugh.

And then and there, walking up and down the room as I often do when thinking hard and talking at the same time, I laid my whole weird theory before him, recapitulating the story of the Brighton Road affairs and picking up my points as I went along, laying special stress upon the reasons which had connected Professor Wolff with them in my mind and keeping nothing back.

Manders proved a splendid listener as he absorbed his brief, so to speak: and I was delighted at the fact that, beyond starting once and raising his eyebrows, he did not turn a hair as I unravelled my fantastic theory. I covered a good deal of ground, recalling much of our talk in Rumania, and spoke for nearly an hour in my anxiety to prove the possibility, if not the probability, of the suggestion I was propounding.

When I stopped and threw myself back in the armchair a trifle exhausted, he gave one long low whistle.

"My God." he said, passing me another cigar almost mechanically: and then he put me through as searching and strenuous cross-examination as ever it has been my lot or most other people's to face.

"Now what do you want me to do?" he asked, when he had concluded, "I do not call you mad, and to my mind you have made out a terribly strong case: and I'm with you to see it Through to the end, however ghastly it may prove. As you say. above all things we must try and forestall worse happenings, if what you surmise be true. No, obviously there is not a moment To be lost,"

"I must stay on the spot and watch any possible developments," I said. " I am convinced that it is my plain and obvious duty, pending the elaboration of a sufficiently strong case to take action upon. Preventive action I shall take myself at all hazards, if all else fail; and then I may require your assistance in your professional capacity if the authorities object subsequently. The situation is so tense at the present juncture That I dare not go away myself and get out of touch, or risk anything delaying my return at the critical moment: so I must fall back on someone else—you, I sincerely trust—to go abroad immediately and make inquiries into the past and the habits of this Professor Lycurgus Wolff of Berlin and Vienna. With your cosmopolitan habit, your knowledge, and your brains, you are the ideal man for my purpose, especially as your inquiries may lead you further afield into the Near East, of which you, like so few people, have a more than superficial knowledge. I hardly like to mention the subject," I added, "but money, either by way of fee or expenses, is no object. I fortunately haven't to worry about that side of things in life, and will draw anything you may want this afternoon."

Manders laughed: and it relieved the situation,

"That's all right, old chap," he struck in. "The cost of a week or two's travel fortunately doesn't matter much to me either, especially as my wife, apart from myself and my earnings, is pretty well off; but I appreciate the thoughtful suggestion. A fee I would not hear of, thank you all the same: but I am your man, and there's my hand on it."

"Thank God" I exclaimed, taking his outstretched hand and wringing it with more feeling than I am usually in the habit of showing—" and thank you! You have taken a great weight off my mind."

"What I can do, I will do, and you may rest assured that I will not spare myself," said Manders, solemnly; "and I am with you to the end of this ghastly business. We will see it through together."

There was a moment of silent reaction, both of us thinking deeply.

"There must be no delay," I said. "It is now the tenth of April, and the thirtieth is Walpurgis Nacht."

Manders gave a little start.

"Yes, I know. I'll start tins very evening by the boat train. Two or three hours, fortunately, will see these beastly proofs through and ready for the printer and then I'll get back home, collect a few things, and appease my wife. She's all right;" he interjected, with a laugh, "a real good sort, who will understand without being told too much, when she gets a hint that it is of vital importance."

"Then, if she does not raise any objection, we might have an early dinner together at the Travellers' and a final Talk," I suggested. "Meanwhile. I will see about tickets, money, etc.- for your journey, and we can have a square up later on. You will at least give me the satisfaction of standing in upon expenses, as I can't go myself?

Manders made a little gesture.

"As you insist then—halves." he agreed: "and I'll leave all that to you. as time presses. My man will take my luggage to the train and see about my seat. And now to work! Don't think me inhospitable in not asking you to lunch, but time won't admit. Mine will be some sandwiches at my writing-table—not for the first time."

"Of course, I understand," I answered, rising. "I'll leave you at once. We will meet at the Travellers' at a quarter to seven. I am most deeply grateful to you, Manders; you have taken an enormous weight off my mind."

"Rot, old chap," was his answer in characteristic English fashion, as he showed me out, "I'm, just as keen as you are to get this whole business cleaned up before any more hell's play takes place."

No words will ever express my relief as I made my way up through the Temple into Fleet Street, and hailed a taxi to take me first to my bank and then to Cook's in Ludgate Circus, and I did not realize that it was two o'clock before I had got all arrangements made, and I was thoroughly hungry.

I drove to the Travellers' and lunched heartily, with a temporary sensation of relief as the result, of my morning's success; and then, during the afternoon. I diligently pursued inquiries as to what was known of Professor Wolff through certain scientific channels open to me, and by calling upon two or three leading men in the scientific world I knew. The result of my investigations proved that, while they knew comparatively little of him personally, his name and his work was; quite familiar to them, and that he had a very considerable reputation. I felt restless, but at the same time so absorbed by the fascination of the business in hand That, rather than seeking the society of friends or acquaintances, I was anxious to avoid anyone to whom I should have to talk upon indifferent or personal subjects.

Eventually I made my way back to The club soon after five and wrote certain letters of introduction for Manders, which might prove helpful. Then I dropped Burgess a line to tell him. that I had seen Manders, and would be back the next afternoon at half-past four, as I had some business to transact in the morning: and I was very glad when my guest turned up sharp on time.

Over dinner and a bottle of old Chambertin I went over the whole groundwork of my case again, and he asked me a good many shrewd questions elucidating details; and I told him about my inquiries of the afternoon.

"You had better go straight through to Berlin and on, in due course, to Vienna," I suggested, "and after that Heaven only knows where your information may take you—farther East in all probability, if you don't find out anything we can go upon. Fortunately The Professor is so well known in the scientific world That it is not like seeking out anyone obscure: and I have got here some letters of introduction which may prove helpful. The one thing, however, that stands out is urgency; and the sooner you are back the better—not later than, say, this day fortnight. Keep me advised by cable if you can; and let me have addresses, whenever possible, in case I require to communicate with you. I leave the contents of your cables to your discretion in view of the alive condition of the local post-office and the fact that the Professor is a local man."

"I shall call the gentleman 'John,' if I refer to him" said Manders, with a laugh, as we drank success to his journey. "There is one good thing however much we may suspect him of the most. extraordinary things, no one will suspect us."

After dinner I handed over the money and the tickets to Manders, together with the letters.

"We'll settle up when you return," I said: and we left it at that.

We were almost silent in the taxi on the way to Charing Cross, as people often are when they have said all that is to be said upon a serious occasion.

Only once Manders spoke.

"By God,'" he burst out, "it seems all too wildly impossible in solemn old foggy London!" I know," I said almost humbly.

"Not but what," he added laying his hand on my arm, "I feel sure that you are right. My instinct tells me so; and, if we succeed—and we shall succeed—you will be instrumental in ridding the world of a ghastly pest, of a most evil thing."

"We, " I said with emphasis, feeling mightily cheered.

Manders' man was waiting at the train by the door of the carriage, everything ready and arranged with the deft correctness of a good body-servant; and I found that Manders was taking him with him.

"Can't do without Pycombe on a journey," he said; with a laugh. "Best courier in Europe, and saves a lazy chap like me no end of bother."

And he waved me good-bye out of the window as though there was no trouble or wickedness in the world, and he were just off on an ordinary vacation jaunt

But I felt the pressure of his final grip, strong and reassuring, long after the boat-train was out of the station.

II

The next morning I spent first at my gun-maker's, going over my guns and testing two or three rifles, which I ordered to be sent down to me without delay at Clymping Manor, together with a couple of Browning automatics, to supplement the one which, as an old traveller, I always carry from long habit. Then I went on to my solicitor and put a few little outstanding matters in order, informing him incidentally that, in the course of the next day or too. I should be bringing or sending him a sealed document under cover to be held on my behalf, but to be taken without a moment's delay to Major Blenkinsopp at Scotland Yard in the event either of my death or of my arrest, I know it sounded rather melodramatic, and he looked at me a bit curiously: but. after ten or twelve years of my unexpectedness, he is getting too case-hardened to offer comment or advice.

It's all right." I said, unable to resist the temptation. "It may be murder this time: and it will be up to you to defend me. Above all, don't forget to brief Fitzroy Manders. I regard him as a very coming man."

And then I made my way back to the club for lunch, stopping on the way to buy a present for Ann—one of those handbags with all sorts of unnecessary bottles that women like to bother themselves with. and the usual chocolates— and two or three boxes of rather special Ramon Allones for old Burgess, who loves a big cigar after dinner.

At the club I picked up a man I hardly knew and made him lunch with me, talking about anything and everything to keep my mind off the real thing and give it a rest.

Dear old faithful Burgess was on the platform, waiting for me: and I could see that he was noticeably relieved at my appearance.

"Well. old chap." I asked, as we greeted each other, "what's the news?

"All well," he replied cheerfully, "but nothing particular to report. Young Bullingdon is much quieter and more rational, though frightfully weak, but can't make out where he is. His mind appears blank about the whole affair and what led up to it. The wounds are going on splendidly, the doctors say. Sir Humphrey has just left: and for the first time he allows himself to take a really hopeful view of the case."

"That's good," I said, as we got into the car. "Perhaps it is the Professor's magic ointment which has worked the cure. How is he, by the by, and what is the news of him?"

"None at all," answered Burgess. "He has not been up again, and I have not been down."

"We must go and return his call one day very soon," I said. speaking lightly, "I came across one or two big scientific folk in town, who tell me that he is a very big man in his own line. It will interest me to see something of

him and his collection, if he will show .it." Then I changed
the subject: "How's Ann?"

"Splendid. She has quite got over the first shock, and is
very interested in the nursing and 'her patient,' as she will
call young Bullingdon, though, naturally, she is not allowed
to do anything for the present at any rate, except run the
'hospital' on the first floor and play at matron."

"Good," I said warmly. "It is a very great thing at the
moment for her to have something to interest her and take
her mind off the awfal side of the whole affair. It is
splendid that she has reacted so well. and shows what a
healthy state she is in mentally as well as physically. And
poor old Mutton and the C.I.D. men?"

"Poor old Mutton." echoed Burgess, with a laugh I was
glad to hear, as he had struck me as a bit overstrained, "he
is like a bear with a sore head; and the C.I.D. men are
kicking .their heels and trying to invent clues."

I smiled a bit grimly in the dusk. I had hardly expected
them to he any further forward if my own theory were
correct. If it were, there was no question of suspicions or
half-measures. It was the whole thing—and a very horrible
thing—or nothing, merely the fantasy of a usually cool and
collected brain running riot as the result of weird
experiences in elemental parts off the beaten track of the
ordinary.

Then came the question I had been fearing, knowing that
Burgess would expect my full confidence, which I was not
prepared to give him for the first time in the history of our
long and intimate friendship.

"And what is your news?" he asked with a nervous
abruptness, which concealed both his eagerness and a
certain umbrage, which I could not but appreciate. "Were
you successful in what you went up to see Manders about?"

"Yes, quite, thank you." I replied, "in so much as I have
enlisted his help: and it has carried things appreciably

forward, if my idea should prove correct. I found him very cordial and receptive; and he went abroad last night at my request upon an important mission in connexion with the business, a thing that neither you nor I could be spared to do at the moment under the existing conditions down here. Don't mention this journey of his to the police or anybody else, by The way."

"Of course I won't," answered Burgess after a pause which was barely noticeable; but I could feel that he, not unnaturally, was annoyed that I showed no sign of taking him fully into my confidence. So we lapsed into silence.

I felt the position quite as keenly as he did, and turned things over m my mind again most carefully:

But it was obvious That I could do no good by burdening him with The details of my bizarre theory, which, to be frank, he was the last person in the world to fall in with. unless substantiated by solid facts and not merely recounted to him like a wild and preposterous chapter out of a hypersensational novel. I knew his limitations and his prejudices as no one else did; and. frankly, he was about The last man I would have chosen in cold blood to make a confidant of in such a matter, especially as he was so nearly concerned in it. It could do no good, and it might even do harm loyal as he was: and it could only make him miserable to go about with the burden of it on his mind.

"Burge, dear old friend." I said at last. breaking the strained silence, as we drew near the house, "you must trust me a little longer and leave me to work this business in the way that seems best to me. I told Manders because Manders can do something immediate to help. At the moment neither you nor I can do anything but await developments which, if I prove correct, cannot be delayed many weeks—most probably not beyond the end of this very month of April. If anything should arise to alter the position and you can do anything, you may rest assured that

I will not delay one hour, not one moment, in telling you the strange idea in my head. To do so prematurely could and would only make you miserable in more ways than one; and, if the whole thing turns out to be only a wild twist of my imagination, I would never forgive myself if I had put it into your mind unnecessarily. We are at the moment faced with a position extraordinary beyond words; and that is my only reason, my only excuse. I hardly know how to express myself. I feel so rotten about the whole thing, which must seem so queer to you. It is on our' old and close friendship that I rely; and on its account I do beg your indulgence to work this thing my own way."

He did not answer immediately: and then there was a certain exasperation in his voice, which. was quite intelligible under the circumstances.

I fail to see," he began . . .

"Yes, of course you do, old chap," I broke in, determined to bring things to a head, "of course you do. Here am I, your oldest pal. staying in your house and treating you, as you think, though it certainly is not so, as a baby. It is very riling; and I quite appreciate that. On the other hand, think of my position. It is equally rotten for me. Surely I can count on you to ascribe the best intentions to me in a difficult position anything but of my own making? Would you prefer me, in the circumstances, to go back to town and await developments there?"

It was the only really strained moment of our year's of friendship: and I played the card purposely trading upon his generosity to appreciate my position.

As the car drove up at The door he held out his hand. "God forbid," he said; and we clasped on it. "I can't understand things: but God knows I trust you as I trust no one else. So I shall just be content to leave things at your discretion."

"Without reservation?" I asked.

"Without reservation." he replied in the old cordial tone: and I must add that during the difficult days that followed, no man could have kept his word more loyally or lessened my own feeling of awkwardness more by his charm of manner, though at times I caught him unawares, frowning and thinking hard with a glim puzzled look on his face. It was a delight to me; and doubled our bond of friendship on my side—if possible.

III

It was with no small pleasure that I heard Jevons say, as he took the things out of the car, that Dorothy Wolff was having tea with Ann; and I noticed Burgess' face light up almost imperceptibly, making me feel more than ever satisfied that I had not yielded to a natural temptation and laid my whole soul bare to him to his distress, rather than risk straining the friendship so dear to me.

For my own reasons I was particularly anxious to study Dorothy Wolff more closely for better, or worse: and here was the opportunity without delay,

Ann, delightful as ever with her wonderful fair hair and white dress, ran across the hall and greeted me with her usual frank sisterly kiss, second only to the one reserved for old Burgess.

"It is good to get you back. Line," she said. "We have missed you horribly: and Burge hasn't known what to do with himself while I have been busy upstairs with the hospital. Where are my chocolates?"

I handed them over to her. I don't think I had missed once since she was a little girl in short frocks and she had begun to regard them as a prescriptive right. In fact, I always used to say that I would not dare return without them.

"Chocolates. Dorothy,'" she said, as I greeted the girl.
"'just at the psychological moment, as superior novelists
say, when we have done tea. Tea, Line. or a drink?"

"Both, please," I said, deliberately expropriating Burgess
and sitting down next to Miss Wolff—"that is, tea first and
the drink some time later, when 1 get stuffy old Burge by
himself sucking at an old pipe and grunting in an
armchair."

They all laughed: and I had created the atmosphere I
wanted. For the next few days it was imperative To keep
things going and permit no brooding.

Dorothy Wolff was looking more charming than ever in
The white fur cap Which suited her so well, yet at the same
time, instinctively raised acute antagonism in me; and I
must admit that I was very much drawn to her personally
by the frankness of her eyes. her direct look which bred
confidence. It gave me to think analytically, if not
furiously, as the old melodramatic Tag has it: and even
frankness is often a disconcerting factor. Somehow—well,
we will get to that later.

"And how is the Herr Professor?" I asked, keeping the
lighter vein. "I have run across one or two of my scientific
friends in town who tell me that he is a wonderful man with
an alphabet of. more than Twenty-six inadequate letters
after his name and the past-master of his own subject."

I noticed Burgess shoot an almost unconscious glance
across at me, as though he suspected the fact that I had
been making inquiries about, the Professor in town; but I
went on cheerfully, as though I had seen nothing.

I am very anxious to pursue the acquaintance, if I may.
Miss Wolff. and would like to call one afternoon and have
a chat with him. What is his best time? I mustn't interrupt
his work on any account."

"Then come in The afternoon," said the girl naturally and
cordially. "He usually goes out for a walk after lunch—or

dinner; as it really is with us—and returns between three and four. So come down with Ann—and Mr. Clymping, too, if he cares to," she added a little shyly, looking across at Burgess— "and stay on to tea. My father is all right when he finds people there and has to talk to them; but if anyone attempts to make an appointment, he always tries on his side to evade it with the instinct of a recluse, a thing which grows upon him more and more each year. So choose "your own afternoon, and come unexpectedly. I am sure to be in, as I go nowhere except here. The very few people who called soon dropped us when they found what a fanny household we are and how unapproachable and irresponsive father is. Only Ann took the trouble to think of me, and be kind to me in my loneliness—and Mr, Clymping."

"That is the drawback of having a genius for a father," I said; and it seemed to me as though she were about to say something. but checked herself sharply. "They can't help having their individualities, which spell peculiarities: and it would be a dull world if we were all turned out of the same ordinary mould, wouldn't it? I rather like eccentric people myself."

"I always regard you as a bit eccentric myself. Line," broke in Ann chaffingly, "with your long disappearances into the unknown. I am always expecting you to turn up with one, if not more coloured wives with their blankets on their backs and a long row of papooses, whatever they are.

"I often wonder where I should put them and what I should feed them on."

"No, never that, my dear Ann, I promise you;" I answered solemnly—"any eccentricity short of matrimony either in the singular or the plural. I swear to you that, if ever I contemplate the greatest adventure of all. I'll bring the poor creature round for your inspection and opinion first; and, more than that unlike most futile folk in love who go

Through this formality, but in their egotism brook nothing but effusive approval, I'll guarantee to abide by your mature and well balanced decision. What are your views upon The subject of marriage. Miss Wolff?"

"I haven't any, to be frank," she answered, looking at me candidly with her big solemn blue eyes. "It is a thing which has never come under my immediate notice."

"Then you are rather like old Burgess here," I said, perhaps a trifle wickedly. "He has kept clear of the snares set for such a charming and eligible young fellow with the imperviousness of a misogynist."

"Don't be an ass. Line," said Burgess, reddening little, to my amusement.

Ann laughed.

"Burge has got me," she said, patting his hand with an air of ownership: "and that ought to be enough for any man."

"Perhaps it will be some day." I said, "if not too much."

"Oh, shut up. Line, I hate you," said the girl. "Have a chocolate to keep you quiet? You are incorrigible. You have come back from town in a very bad mood. What did you do with yourself?"

"Nothing I couldn't tell you or any other nice young girl in her teens," I replied. "I went to see my lawyer and made a codicil to my will, leaving you an annuity of chocolates; and, talking of lawyers, I renewed my acquaintance with Fitzroy Manders and took him to dinner at the club, a carnal joy which appeals much more to sensible men. of our age than all your unsubstantial fantasies of love and sugary sentiment."

"A very nice man," said Ann. "You might have done much worse. 'I liked him very much; he is so clever."

There was nothing in our tea-table talk, as we babbled on—purposely lightly on my part: but it served my object, and gave me the chance I wanted of drawing out Dorothy Wolff and forming my own opinion of her. Candidly it was

all, more than all, in her favour. She was charmingly frank
and unaffected: and nothing could lurk behind the complete
candour of those solemn blue eyes. In fact, she was as
unsophisticated as a child; and the real wonder was that she
was so fresh and natural considering the strangeness of her
surroundings. And I felt more than ever that it was up to me
to penetrate The mystery that lay behind it all— if I were
not mistaken, the victim of an hallucination of my own
deliberate creation.

Then came The old question which has broken up so
many happy interludes in life,

What is the time?" The girl asked, as the grandfather
clock in the hall chimed.

"A quarter to six," answered Burgess reassuringly; "but
it's all right. I told Wilson to leave the car at the door. and
I'll drive you home; so you won't be late,"

The girl gave him a grateful look, and it struck me how
typical it was of Burgess' thoughtfulness of detail for
others, and what a good husband he would make when the
time came for me to stand beside him at the chancel rails as
his best man, Ann and I saw them off; and then I lit a cigar.

"You shall play me something nice and thoughtful and
soothing, Ann," I said, "if you don't think it will disturb the
hospital or reach the Bullingdon ward. It's so nice to be
home." And I settled myself down in a big chair in front of
the fire and was soon deep in thought, while Ann, knowing
my habits, played on by instinct just what I wanted without
my realizing particularly what it was. Such music helps to
co-ordinate thought.

IV

The next three days, much to Burgess' disgust—and
Ann's, too, for that matter—I was busy writing. It was the
document for my solicitor and, ultimately, Scotland Yard,

covering the possibilities ahead and working out my Theory in detail on paper. It was difficult writing in a way, but it helped me more than I was aware of in many respects to put the thing on paper in a logical, well-elaborated fashion, giving my reasons and references, scientific and personal: and, apart from acting as a covering document in certain eventualities—a precaution. I may add, many doctors and other persons placed in strange anomalous positions would often be well advised to take—it not only relieved my mind from the point of view of regularizing the irregular as far as humanly possible, but served to convince me more than ever, in my own mind, that I had hit upon no wild fantasy, no bizarre hallucination, no lunatic theory, but the key to the weirdest and most gruesome thing that had ever befallen sedate old England in these latter days of alleged civilization, which is. after all, only the conventional veneer adopted to cover the primitive that is in us all, be it deep down or near the surface.

The conviction that I was correct, however, despite the relief of having finished my unwelcome task, left a dull weight behind it: and I blotted the last page with a heavy anxious heart in view of what I felt was ahead, just as it was time to dress for dinner on Sunday, the third day of my self imposed task, which Ann believed to be a dry-as-dust contribution to one of the big reviews.

Burgess, I could see, knew better, though, sportsman that he always is, he made my task easier by never saying a word, far less asking a question. I admired his splendid loyalty, under the circumstances, more than I can ever say, as I know what it all meant to him, and how inwardly he was irked by this atmosphere of secrecy and reserve, which he naturally could not appreciate.

At dinner that night I announced my intention of running up to town the next day. I felt, though I did not say so, that after all, I hardly dared trust my document to the post, even though registered, and would prefer to deliver it into my solicitor's hands myself. It was not a thing to risk falling into anyone else's hands at the moment: and it was not worth leaving such a thing to chance, small as the danger really was.

Ann made a face of disappointment; and Burgess looked up quickly.

"I'll drive you up, if you like," he offered; "and we can come back after lunch. I want to go to my tailor."

"It's awfully good of you," I answered noncommittally. "We'll talk it over later on."

But over our last cigar I told him frankly that I could not risk his being away even for the inside of a day, in case anything should happen; and he nodded without a word. perhaps not displeased in a way to think he was essential after all. Once Burgess has made up his mind, there never was a fellow like him to play the prescribed game, whatever it might be, down to the most meticulous detail without question or reproach: and in this great tragic game in which we were involved he had accepted me as captain. I went up by the morning train, deposited my document lunched at the club, and was back again at four-thirty, with Burgess on the platform to meet me—this time with no inconvenient questions.

V

During the days just covered all had gone smoothly, and without hitch or complication both indoors and out—greatly to my relief, but for certain reasons not altogether contrary to my expectation.

The best of accounts came from The "hospital" of young Bullmgdon's progress: and not only was he pronounced quite out of danger, but gaining strength and making progress, though no one had been allowed to see or question him for fear of throwing him back. His extreme weakness and the mental reaction made him apathetic; and he did not seem to worry, sleeping long recuperative hours, taking his nourishment without question, and satisfied simply to be where he was without undue questioning. His system, both mentally and physically, had been exhausted by the delirium; but youth was obviously asserting itself, and Sir Humphrey promised that in a day or two, if all went well, possibly Major Blenkinsopp might see him for a few minutes and talk to him more in the guise of a new doctor than as a detective.

The delirium had quite gone, and his mind seemed a blank with regard to "the big dog with green eyes jumping over the moon," or any such seeming absurdities of an uncontrolled mind; and he had not even mentioned Miss St. Chair. The nurses, however, reported that he had once or twice, during the time I was in town, worn a puzzled look and appeared as though he wanted to ask a question; but from the inertia of absolute weakness he had apparently let things slide and relapsed into a state of contentment.

He had recognized Sir Humphrey Bedell, whom he had known all his life. and had smiled when he told him to lie still and be a good boy, adding that he had been very ill, but was in the best of hands and doing well. He had also told him to ask no questions, but had deputed Burgess or myself to see him if he grew restless and worried.

So far, so good; but I felt morally certain that there could be nothing to be learnt from him that would help things forward. Whatever it was, it had obviously all been too sudden and complete for him to tell us more than we knew already.

With regard to the Professor I had not been, for my own reasons, anxious to hurry things in the absence of Manders or any report from him or—of fresh developments, shall I say? Above all, I was anxious not to make this strange recluse suspicious by any sign of eagerness that I had any but a purely scientific interest in him. A recluse by the very essence of things resents intrusion, and this natural resentment of itself breeds unnatural suspicion: and such people, especially in the position in which I found myself placed, have to be approached ostensibly casually, yet with the utmost tact. Moreover, beyond studying his habits and personality in his own chosen surroundings, in his case, too, I felt I could really do little that was practical until the time for action came—the psychological moment that Ann had made fun of—when action would of necessity be short and sharp to be decisive and successful. Therefore, it was essential to lay all my lines with scrupulous care. Nevertheless, I was by no means sony to find Dorothy Wolff again at tea. and took the opportunity to arrange dial we would all drop in casually the following afternoon and stay to tea.

The more I saw of The girl. the more I liked her, I must admit: but there were still things I could not quite understand or reconcile. Of the fact that Burgess had at last fallen a victim to the oldest commonplace in the world's history, which to each individual pair seems the height both of originality and bliss, I felt no longer in doubt: yet, much as I liked Dorothy personally. God knows there was much at The back of my mind to make me strangely worried and anxious as to The outcome of his passion, which, quiet and unobtrusive as it was, would, I knew, prove a very strong and virile thing, overriding all difficulties and objections, and lifelong in its reaction if things went agley. It was a constant thought that lived with me after I had realized the fact itself: yet, awful as I knew the intermediate stage must be, I felt with a strange totally illogical optimism that somehow, by some means—by the grace of God— it would come right in the end.

And thus Dorothy was after all the principal reason why I dared not, would not take my dearest and oldest friend into my confidence, until fate. fortified by facts, forced my hand: and I had a fear at the back of my mind at times lest she might, after all, be destined—even temporarily—to come between Burgess and myself after so many years of such close intimacy and understanding with never a cloud, far less a quarrel, to look back on. Yet, as I have said. I was nevertheless strangely drawn to Dorothy, the rock of danger upon which our treasured friendship might split and find shipwreck, as so often the case with a woman and two men, even where there has been neither jealousy nor competition: and I could not persuade myself that destiny, with all its spite and freakishness, held anything but friendship for Dorothy and myself. But in the background of it all lurked the unknown quantity that might make shipwreck of the happiness of all of us; and at best, she was destined to suffer much before we could any of us hope to take up the threads of life and face a future of happiness. But the ordeal would be short and sharp in its denouement.

Burgess again took the opportunity of driving her home; and Ann laughed happily.

"I believe it has happened at last," she said; "and do you know, Line, I believe I should have been horribly jealous of any other girl?"

I nodded solemnly, preoccupied by my thoughts.

"What an old bear you are!" exclaimed the girl. "I must say I don't envy any girl who gets you as her lot in life. You haven't a spark of romance in your whole make-up. Yet, after all, I believe I should be frantically jealous of her somehow—in a purely platonic way—from force of habit and old association, I suppose."

"My dear child," I replied, recovering my gaiety, "I am a crusty curmudgeon who would certainly be fated to make any romantic young girl abysmally unhappy: so I shall forgo the doubtful pleasure of a personal dip into the matrimonial lucky-tub and play godfather to the lot of you—pantomimes, silver mugs, and all the rest of it."

"Shut up," said Aim, taking my arm, "and come and have a game of billiards."

VI

The next morning Burgess had to go to the farthest corner of the estate to see about some repairs; and I cried off, pleading laziness and the fact that I had promised to drive into Crawley with Ann, who wanted to do some household shopping.

It was a glorious morning, and Ann looked radiant as I took my place beside her in her own special two-seater—a Rover similar to The one in which the poor Bolsovers, who in their newly married happiness and joy of life had always made a special appeal to my imagination, had met their ghastly fate, as I read it, growing more and more certain in my own mind every day of what really had happened.

Ann was in specially high spirits at the excellent news from the "hospital"; and the nurses had allowed her to peep round the screen at "her" patient while he lay there sleeping.

"So pale. Line. and so frail." she said. looking at me in her frank sisterly fashion, "but so nice, looking, bandages and all. My whole heart went out to the poor boy lying there; and I can't tell you how it bucks me up—horrid word, isn't it, but expressive—to get such good accounts of him. You see, it was I who found him and gave him 'first aid'; so I was his first nurse, and he is really my patient, I consider, and I always tell the nurses so, whatever they may think? They only laugh and say that, as soon as Sir Humphrey will allow it, they will dress me up in uniform and send me in as the new nurse to take rny turn.'"

I laughed. It was so like Ann and what I loved about her. Besides that. it was one of God's own mornings, when one wanted to sing, if it had not for a reservation at the back of one's mmd. The sun was high in the heavens: but was all well with the world?

"Oh, Ann dear. you're a perfect darling," I cried. "If you weren't you, I would never know whether you were ingenuous or ingenious! God bless your innocence and keep the 'u' where the 'i' is with most girls in tills day and generation."

"Whatever do you mean. Line?" she asked, half-puzzled. "You always talk like a bad actor out of a worse play."

"I mean I'd many you myself, my one and only Ann," I answered, "if I weren't old enough to be your grandfather and so horribly fond of you—the absurdly mistaken reason for which so many futile folk face a parson in full uniform on a weekday, and agree to make each other mutually miserable for life."

"It takes two, if not more, to a marriage, my good Line," she replied, making an eleven-year-old face at me, which recalled so many happy days. "And now here we are at the butcher's, where all problems are practical and still-life is served out automatically by the pound and the ounce; so a truce to cynicism and love alike. What shall I get?"

"Devilled kidneys," I replied, as I helped her out.

"You've got to catch your kidney first at a country butcher's," she called back over her shoulder, as she entered the shop.

I waited on the pavement, watching the butchery assistant cutting off a very large piece of topside, as I lit a cigarette.

"You've got a fine show of meat," I said casually, by way of making conversation; "and that's a healthy lump for a large family."

It's for a very small family, as it happens, sir," the man replied, "Its for That old German professor up at the Dower

House. He eats a wonderful lot of meat, and very little else: and they do say he eats it mostly raw."

I started involuntarily. Chance was bringing extraordinary little details to light—tiny corroborations all piecing into one big whole: and again I knew that, for all its bizarreness, that my weird theory was the correct solution, and I was determined to go ahead without allowing myself to be put off or diverted an inch either to the right hand or to the left.

"People talk a parlous lot of nonsense in the country," I said as lightly as I could," especially about foreigners."

And I turned the talk on to other things, wondering, incidentally, that the vagaries of yokel public opinion had not fastened upon the strange old Teuton recluse in connexion with the Brighton Road mysteries for lack of anything more definite.

And then out came Ann triumphant, with the butcher's boy following with kidneys and a basket-full of other things, and took me off to give the grocer a turn.

VII

After lunch and a game of billiards we started off on our projected visit to the Dower House, walking through the gardens to the wood, and examining the progress of Ann's pet bulbs, just as Burgess and she had done exactly a fortnight before on the memorable day on which they had chanced upon young Bullingdon; and, as on that day. Whiskers trotted along gaily beside us with a terrier's joy of living on a fine afternoon.

"What's that parcel you've got there. Line?'" asked Ann. " Something for the Professor?"

"No, my curious child," I replied, "only a box of chocolates for your blue-eyed Dorothy. It was really intended for you one day when you were good or looked

hungry, or tumbled down and hurt your knee—that is, if
you still have such things, though we don't see so much of
them as we used to: but I thought it would be nice to take it
to Miss Wolff instead, as I don't suppose down in your out-
of-the-way old Dower House very many come her way,"

"Very thoughtful of you, dear Line—at my expense!"
laughed Ann, "What a good thing I'm not so greedy as you
used to make me!"

We turned into the dense wood: and. when we came to
the place where young Bullingdon had been found.
Whiskers showed signs of eagerness to explore, and had to
be called to heel.

"He always gets excited now when we get near here."
said Burgess, patting him. "He doesn't seem to he able to
get over his discovery, and is inordinately proud of the big
part he played. Good dog- good dog."

The last to Whiskers, who looked up and wagged his tail
frantically, coming on after us with a wistful look back
from time To time,

Then we struck off to the right where the path forked, and
began to descend between the dense trees. These had been
to an extent cleared round the house itself, which was
officially approached by a drive through the wood on the
other side, and lay in a gloomy garden, disproportionately
small for its importance, with only patches of sun-light
amidst the prevailing shadow.

The whole atmosphere was one of dampness amongst the
trees, and there were one or two big pools to the side of the
track as we drew near to the little slip-gate into the woods:
and I noticed Whiskers, who trotted up and sniffed one,
shake his head and run off, whining as though frightened. I
purposely made no remark, but went across, as though
casually, and examined it, The water had a strange,
unpleasant appearance—turgid, with a strange lurid sparkle
of it's own out of keeping with the shadow around, as

though the water itself held some strange individual life within it: and it had a peculiar. though not very strong odour, which was quite distinctive.

At the gate I rejoined Ann and Burgess, bending down to pat Whiskers reassuringly, knowing how susceptible a dog is—in fact most, if not all, animals are—to the human touch when frightened; and he looked up into my face and began again to cock his tail and wag it.

"No wonder your Georgian ancestor sacrificed architecture to hygiene and sunshine, Burgess," I said, glad that neither of them appeared to have noticed anything strange about either the clog or myself: "and you ought to be grateful to him for risking the accusation of vandalism or swank, and building for his descendants a fine airy hill-top abode in the sun. And he certainly wasn't a vandal either, as the house he built is the perfection of the period," I added lightly—the atmosphere I wanted to preserve at all costs. "I wonder that you don't scrap some of your personal artistic instincts, and at least clear' off all the trees for a good distance round and give the sun a chance, even in such a hollow, of burning out the dampness."

Burgess laughed. "I have often thought of it, but somehow hated the idea—silly prejudice in these days, I suppose: but I must admit that it seems to have grown worse of late, more oppressive somehow and a trifle mouldy. I'll talk To the Professor about it."

VIII

And So we passed into the garden: and somehow I could appreciate his feeling with the true American's love of the tradition we so largely lack in our own lives and surroundings, as I looked upon the low, mulhon-windowed house with its stone court and big old stone barn to the right, the sole remnant the original Clymping Castle with

its historic memories. Beyond the barn was a glimpse of
old red wall, such as folk can't grow nowadays—and
Americans envy—- concealing the kitchen garden beyond,
which lay to the right of the front garden and got more so,
but not much withal.

The whole place wore an air of neglect, quite different
from the last time I had seen it; and did not tend to cheer
one, especially in my particular mood.

"Damned bad tenant you've got anyhow; Burgee I said a
trifle caustically, 'The place looks and smells horribly
neglected."

Burgess laughed a little awkwardly, if not apologetically.

"The Professor does not keep a gardener," he said. "I
suppose he doesn't understand our ways. I must send one of
the men down to tidy up a bit. and suggest to him to get
someone."

I made no further comment, realizing the psychology of
the situation and knowing how much more it must irk tidy,
methodical, agricultural old Burgess than my casual self.
But obviously he did not want to quarrel with his tenant's
shortcomings for private reasons.

We made our way round the house and found Dorothy at
the front ostensibly gardening, but in reality waiting for our
arrival.

She advanced a trifle flushed and more beautiful than
ever, taking off a pair of muddy gloves as she held out her
hands to Ann and kissed her.

"This is indeed kind of you all," she said. greeting
Burgess and myself more discreetly. "I am tidying up a bit
and admiring all the bulbs, not only the ones that are in
bloom, but those coming on. I love tulips—great tall
Darwin tulips, like regiments of Guards with all sorts of
wonderful coloured head-dresses. One begins to get tired of
white and yellow as the spring goes on and summer
approaches."

"You will find plenty of them here. Miss Wolff," said Burgess eagerly, "and I will tell you where all the different sorts are and what colours to expect. Ann and I love them, too; and it is a hobby of ours to work out designs and colour schemes. Next month you will find them a picture; and you will love ours up at the Manor, I'm sure."

I gave the pair a little moment of their own, the old prelude to the love song—without words; or with words used to disguise intention, which Talleyrand diagnosed to be their proper use in this wicked world.

Then I broke in, greeting my hostess.

"From the sublime to the succulent. Miss Wolff! I have brought you a box of chocolates, and shall be so glad if you'll relieve me of them my arm is getting tired with carrying them."

"It is kind of you, Mr. Osgood," said the girl, turning to me: "and what a big box! It will last me weeks and weeks. A year ago I would have eaten them in a day or two; but somehow, in my old age, I am not nearly so fond of sweet things as I used to be."

Again I started, mentally more than physically. Strange ideas surged up, one confirming another: and this one was fraught with a strange mixture of disturbance, touched with a certain assurance.

"Ann will always help," I said, laughing nevertheless.

Another thing I had noticed which gave me an unpleasant qualm—almost a feeling of nausea. At her breast Dorothy Wolff was wearing a weird orange flower covered with hideous black protruding spots, which suggested more than anything else some particularly noxious disease—a flower the like of which I would dare have bet had never been seen in England before,

The beastly thing; fraught with ill omen, irritated my nerves beyond all words: and I felt that I must take some action to relieve my feelings, as I could not spend the whole afternoon with its offensiveness under my nose.

Meanwhile, the conversation had become general: and we began to stroll round the garden, Burgess telling Dorothy about the bulbs and pointing out the different names and colours that were due to reveal themselves the following month. I was silent, wondering how I could get the girl alone for a moment, when chance, as so often in fact as well as in fiction, came to my rescue.

"Oh. look there, Burge." cried Ann, pointing to the hedge that divided the garden to the left of the house from a field, "some big animal has made a hole in the hedge—a cow, I suppose. It will want seeing to; or they will be straying into the garden and doing damage to the beds. It's just by dear old granny's favourite herbaceous border, too."

And with proprietorial instinct they both moved off to examine the damage.

I seized the opportunity without beating about the bush.

"Wherever did you get that flower?" I asked abruptly.

"My father gave it to me," she answered. "With his peculiar scientific tastes he seems rather to admire them, though he treats all flowers as mere specimens, so far as that goes."

"Wherever did he get it from?" I asked, with something deeper than idle curiosity.

"Oh, he brought some roots from the Balkans with him to see if they would grow in this country." she replied without any reserve: "and this is one of the first results—small but satisfactory; he says."

"Where are they?" I asked; and she led me across to a damp corner of the garden under some tall trees.

There was a small hollow; and in it a small puddle of the same queer water. Whiskers, who had Stuck close to me as though for protection since I had patted him, again began to whine and grow restive; and I had to pat him reassuringly once more. Then he turned tail and ran across to Burgess.

Round the banks of the hollow were growing other flowers like The one at the girl's breast, though not so far out in bloom—not only this hideous orange variety with its black spots, but vivid white and some red ones as well.

"May I examine yours?" I said. holding out my hand.

She took it from her breast and handed it to me without demur; and I took it and examined its orange and black hideousness carefully. It had a faint and sickly smell, subtly suggestive of death, and from its stalk oozed a sticky white sap.

"Of the snapdragon family," I said quietly.

Then I threw it, apparently impulsively, upon the ground and crushed it under my heel. "Ugh, what a damnable thing! It makes me positively sick."

Then I made as though to recover myself, as I saw a half-look of fear in her eyes.

"Oh, I am sorry. Miss Wolff," I apologized. "Can you forgive my rudeness?"

"Yes," she answered, taking no offence and speaking with more truth than she knew, "you meant no harm: but my father . . ,"

"Your father? Yes, please don't tell him I destroyed one of his botanical experiments: he would never forgive me. For my sake you must pretend you lost it: you needn't say how."

We heard Ann and Burgess coming up from behind to join us, and we turned to meet them before she could reply; but I had gathered the fact from the sudden look in her eyes that she was afraid of the saturnine old Professor, and my heart went out to her with a redoubled determination to shield her, if not too late, from the horrible doom that was hanging so closely over her head. But it was a heart doubly heavy for Burgess's sake.

"Yes, some animal has broken through." called out Burgess, as we walked forward to meet them, leaving the ill-omened hollow behind us. "I must speak to Hedges or Recce about it, and have it fixed up some time but at present there are no beasts of any sort in the field."

"What wonderfully quick eyes you have got, Ann," I said, again getting on to the lighter tack essential to the salvation of the situation. "Thank the Lord I'm not your husband; or I should be afraid to come into the house with my boots on the country, or to go out for the evening on my own in town."

"My dear Line," she answered, in a tone of assumed haughtiness; "if you laid your face and your fortune—and your face is certainly not your fortune, I may add—at my feet, wild automobiles would never drag me like a lamb to the altar. People soon get tired of chocolates; and they are your only excuse or saving grace in my life,"

"Did you ever hear such a couple for nagging at other?" laughed Burgess To Dorothy. "They really ought to be married; and I believe that old Solomon would refuse a decree nisi from his appreciation of the fitness of things, and his wonderfully sardonic sense of humour."

IX

We were approaching the houses and my eyes ran over it with a sense of deep affection, half-love of architecture and half-sympathy with Burgess—a masterpiece in miniature, an epitome of tradition. But I think what had always fascinated me most was the wide, massive, rather squat front door of fifteenth-century oak, windswept by Sussex sou'-westers for close on four hundred years, and studded with great nails of iron. Round it was a weather-beaten stone arch, surmounted by the old Clympynge arms over the door upon a stone shield, almost erased by the tooth of time—a bend with three escallops charged upon it, between six bulls' heads cabossed, with the motto "Ascendo" underneath—supposed to be an example of heraldic word-play, falsely connecting the name of Sir Burgess de Clympynge, The Norman founder of the family, with the word "climbing."

But somehow that afternoon—April 16 according to my diary—even with The afternoon sun aslant across its mellow brick, it seemed almost to have assumed some sinister aspect, and the old mullioned windows to frown— imagination, of course, and overwrought nerves, ever on the strain beneath a light exterior and cloak of carelessness, but nevertheless hard to shake off.

And the unpleasant impression was not lightened of any of its sinister suggestion when the old familiar door was opened, with a clanking and the rattle of the chain, by the old German-Polish servant, Anna Brunnolf, whom I had not seen before——a strange figure with her slanting eyes and towsled grey hair, wearing her habitual cape of brown fur. She was not only bizarre in herself and so utterly out of the picture, but there was something about her that gave me a sort of "gooseflesh" feeling. There was an aura of evil, of repulsion, round her to those sensitive to such intangible influences, as I have always been since I can first remember: and she made no effort to welcome us, closing the door behind us, locking it again, and putting up the old chain with an attitude suggestive of hostility.

"That's one of Anna's fads," said Dorothy, trying to speak lightly. "It has grown on. her through living in wild parts of recent years with my nomadic father."

Whiskers had made no effort to follow us in, nor had Anna given him either encouragement or chance: and to Burgess's surprise, when we got home that evening, we found him lying in front of the hall fire, strangely out of spirits and apologetic for his desertion. I made no comment at The time. but felt that there was a special bond of understanding and sympathy between the dog and myself.

There was no fire in the old oak-panelled hall with its big open fireplace, which had in the old days blazed with big logs and a cheerful glow of welcome, lighting up the armorial shield over the stone arch, this time striking a richer note with its heraldic colourings—azure, a bend gules with the three escallops argent charged upon it, between six bulls' heads cabossed or. There was no reflection from it either, as of old, upon thc minstrcl gallery in miniature opposite, or the old oak staircases and in the deepening light, through the leaded windows, it looked forlorn and cheerless—almost dour.

Moreover, without the great fire that had burnt for centuries of winters disguising it, its dampness lay revealed: and it was dank and musty with the suggestion of a charnel-house. Again, it seemed to me that there was a slight, almost imperceptible odour of strange decay. faint, yet to me strangely pungent. There was a blight, a gloom over the whole place; and I could not repress a slight shiver as we found ourselves out of the sunlight.

Dorothy seemed to notice it, and spoke half-apologetically. "Come into the drawing-room. It's always nice and cheerful in There with a big fire—I see to that. Anna won't be bothered with a lot of fires or have any help: and father and she don't seem to notice things as I do, as they both keep up their habit of wearing furs. acquired during severe winters in the Balkans and other such places, regardless of the fact that we are in England. And Anna has put away such a lot of Mr. Clymping's beautiful furniture and nice things in unused bedrooms with sheets over them, like dead bodies, to save trouble and work. Ugh, it all gives me creeps, though I am accustomed to it," she concluded, leading the way to the drawing-room. " I love light and fires and lots of lovely things everywhere. I often feel that I was made for them, though I have had so little chance of having them—so far,"

It was unconsciously pathetic.

I caught a glimpse of Burgess's face with the sunlight across it. His eyes were fixed intently upon the beautiful girl: and it seemed to me that I could read both displeasure with the present state of things and the unspoken intention of doing all that lay in his power to give her the surroundings she craved for. I could not. however, help wondering, had things been otherwise, how Burgess would have felt and acted towards tenants who treated his intensely venerated ancestral home in such a careless and cavalier fashion, lacking not only artistic appreciation, but even common consideration.

X

A few minutes later the door opened abruptly; and in came the saturnine old professor, crossing the room with his long characteristic stride, his strange eyes. under their shaggy, slanting brows, fixing upon each one of us in turn none too kindly, and looking through us half-suspiciously. I took his hand. with the long pointed fingers, and gripped it with apparent heartiness, looking him back straight in the eyes.

"I have availed myself of your kind invitation to come and have a scientific chat wifh you, Professor," I said; "and I trust that I have not come at an inconvenient time."

Professor Wolff mastered his disinclination with an effort, and did his best to welcome me.

"I am delighted to meet anyone interested in my subjects," he replied." It is so rare in Sussex. Come into my room; and leave these young people to discuss the sort of tilings that interest them."

He took me into the library, which looked as though it had not been dusted since his arrival. It was both musty and dusty, with the furniture all awry, odd tables of all periods collected from various parts of the house and piled with open books, bundles of notes, specimens, and all the paraphernalia of a student and a bookworm.

A small fire smouldered on the hearth, and he stirred it impatiently and threw a couple of big logs on before throwing himself down on a big sofa and curling himself up like a dog, with his legs half under him, in one comer, motioning to me to seat myself, as he drew up a great grey fur rug over the lower part of his long body.

He was a most wonderful man, unpleasant as he was personally and abhorrent physically; and he had a rare and marvellous brain. I shall never forget that hour with him, sitting opposite to him, fascinated not only by his ceaseless talk upon recondite subjects which were obviously everyday commonplaces to him, but by his extraordinary personality, which, above all things, I had come to study; and the only thing was that the one warred with the other and divided my attention, while he watched me the whole time intently, yet withal furtively and with shifty eyes, as I listened to the rough, guttural sentences pouring fiom him like a scientific avalanche.

I can hardly say whether I was glad or sorry when Dorothy tapped on the door and nervously announced that tea was ready. It broke the spell but I had accomplished the real object of my visit, and my last lingering doubt—if any there had been—had vanished as to the inwardness of the strange genius, with whom I had sat in such close proximity all alone in the fading light—a weird experience in the twentieth century for one who knew the horrible truth the whole time.

"Come," he said abruptly, as though the spell had been broken, "we must go back to your friends as they will be anxious to be leaving before the light entirely departs."

The drawing-room was bright and cheerful, a pleasant contrast; which I welcomed with every fibre of my body. Even my intellect felt surcharged.

I stood by Dorothy while she poured out the tea, the Professor standing on the hearthrug and talking intermittently to Burgess with his mouth full as he greedily devoured sandwich after sandwich—a most unpleasing sight.

"I do not know whether you dainty English will care for my special sandwiches," he remarked truculently. "I have them made of raw meat. Some of our leading professors in Germany advocate them; and they are given to invalids as they are so strengthening and so easily"—he paused for an instant for the word, munching the while—"what you call assimilated. I find my brain works much better on them. Once you folk got over your' silly ideas and prejudices you would find that they are delicious—much better than your dry, tough, scorched meat. I am teaching Dorothea to eat them."'

I looked at the girl a trifle anxiously.

"Yes," she said without affectation; "and I hope you won't Think it horrid of me, but I am quite beginning to like them. though they don't seem very dainty, and I have never eaten them in public, I have always looked at them from the scientific or medical point of view."

I saw the Professor's eyes fixed furtively upon her.

"Where is the flower that I gave you, Dorothea?" he asked across the room, in a rough, angry voice.

She put her hand instinctively to her breast and looked down.

"I—I must have lost it," she answered, flushing.

"You are very careless," began The old man with something that sounded very much like a snarl; and then he broke off, as though conscious of his visitors.

One Thing was certain in my mind—to my relief—at any rate he was not suspicious, and never dreamt that perhaps people were even then hovering upon the fringe of his horrid secret.

I turned to the girl, asking for a second cup of tea to cover any awkwardness, feeling that she was afraid of the old German, who was obviously an autocrat and a bit of a bully in his own household.

"Thank you for not giving me away," I said in a low voice, as Burgess began to speak about sending one of his men down to tidy up. "Is your name really 'Dorothea' and not 'Dorothy?' "

"My father always calls me by the German form—perhaps not unnaturally," she answered; "but my mother always used to call me 'Dorothy.'"

"Your mother?" I asked sympathetically.

"She died when I was quite a little girl," she answered very softly, as though not wishing to be overheard and nursing something very sacred to herself. " I always like to call myself Dorothy and to be called Dorothy by my friends, as it reminds me of her."

"May I call you Dorothy?" I asked upon impulse.

"If you care to." she answered, with a little look of friendly confidence, which was much in my mind during the next few urgent anxious days.

I was glad and relieved when we found ourselves once more out in the open air, and I heard old Anna shoot the bolts and clank the chain behind us, though my heart was very heavy for the poor doomed girl inside—doomed unless by the grace of God she could be saved from a fate too hideous to contemplate: and I was not very talkative on the way home, as we hurried as well as we could through the dark wood, which had grown so strangely oppressive to me.

When we reached the Terrace I drew a deep breath of relief and filled my lungs with the crisp, clean air.

"You are lucky to live up here on the hill, old chap," I said to Burgess, speaking from the bottom of my heart: but all the evening I was depressed, though I did my best to conceal it, and somehow I did not seem able to get the unpleasant odour of decay out of my nostrils.

XI

The next morning brought strange news.

As we were smoking in the hall over the papers after breakfast, Jevons announced our old friend Mutton; and Burgess ordered him to be shown in at once.

"Dirty work on the downs last night- gentlemen," he announced solemnly, "but nothing like as serious as before—no connexion with the other in fact. Two of Farmer Stiles's sheep have been killed and mutilated on the downs."

"That's bad business," said Burgess, with a low whistle. "What do you.make of it?"

I made no remark. My only feeling was one of relief, in a way, that it was nothing worse.

"It looks something like that Great Wyrley business up Staffordshire," answered Mutton, pleased to have a theory. "Both are torn, badly lacerated, and partially disembowelled: and it looks like some devil's mischief."

Yes, thats just what it is," I rejoined, "sheer wanton devil's mischief, inspector, without apparent object. We will come along with you and have a look at it."

It was four or five miles away; so Burgess ordered the car, and it was not long before we were on the spot.

"Looks as if they had been worried by some big dogs," said Burgess; and I assented, purposely not taking any very marked interest or advancing any theory of my own.

"You don't know of any savage dog or other big animal in the neighbourhood?" I asked Mutton casually.

"No," he answered, shaking his head; "but I will put my men on to search. It looks as though, some lads or young ruffians had set something on to worry the poor brutes."

"And the rest of the flock?" I asked.

"Oh, they were evidently frightened out of what little wits sheep have, and were found no end of a way off, all huddled together and sort of dazed, if you can say such a thing of a sheep. Farmer Stiles has had them all driven into a field near his house."

We had a talk with the farmer, who could throw no light on the subject; and then, as we turned to go home. I saw the new moon for the first time from the top of the downs, and I calculated that it was the third day.

I gazed at it without remark, fascinated at the thought of the possibilities of horror with which it was fraught. Why should the moon have such a malign influence, I asked myself? Was it soured virginity, or revenge for the havoc Endymion had wrought?

And each day and night after that I watched her growing crescent approaching full face, wondering each time what it was going to bring forth.

XII

Thursday and Friday passed without event, everything going well on the surface; and we seemed to he living through beautiful spring days without a worry or a horror in the world, especially in dear old sleepy Sussex.

Bullingdon made capital progress and gave the doctors every cause for satisfaction; and on Saturday morning he was so much better that he began to worry, and expressed a desire to see his host. He was insistent; and Ann came down to Burgess and myself and told us. In view of Sir Humphrey Bedell's contingent permission and The state of the patient, the nurses considered that it would do no harm—in fact, that it would do more good than harm, as it would keep him from worrying.

"All right, dear," said Burgess, rising, "I'll go up."

Then once more I intervened, a little awkwardly.

"It is a strange thing to ask even of such an old friend in his own house," I said, laying my hand on his arm, "and I don't want to appear to take too much upon myself: but do you mind if I am the first to see him? I have my own particular reasons."

Burgess looked at me for a moment in surprise—a little chagrined. I thought—and I must confess that I was more than a trifle uncomfortable in view of the secretive attitude I had felt compelled to take up.

"His first impressions may be valuable to my theory," I explained—"the theory upon which I build so much to clear up the whole of this ghastly business. More depends upon it than perhaps you can ever guess."

"All right, old chap," came his prompt reply: and I don't think I have ever admired his character and his staunchness so much. It made me more than ever determined to repay him if it lay in my power—if by my instrumentality his life's happiness could be secured.

"Thank you," was all I dared say at the moment, however: and I went straight upstairs.

Young Bullingdon was looking frail, but he had made wonderful progress the last day or two; and I took his hand and sat down near him.

"You mustn't worry, Lord Bullingdon," I Said reassuringly. "You are in good hands and making splendid progress."

"What has happened?" He asked in a puzzled voice.

"You had a bad accident with your big car and have been lying between life and death for over a fortnight."

"I don't remember anything about it," he said blankly.

It was as I expected I might almost say, hoped.

The shock, as in so many cases of sudden and severe accident, had left his mind a complete blank with regard to the event; and perhaps, in the circumstances it was better, if memory upon the point returned at all, that it should be later rather than sooner, when he would be both physically and mentally better able to bear the shock. In some cases on record shock has cut memory clean off at a point long before and often totally unconnected with the accident; and I was anxious particularly to test the reaction in this case.

"What do you remember last?" I inquired, speaking casually. "Supper, or dinner, or something of the sort—at Brighton, I think," he answered confusedly." I can't be quite sure. It makes my head ache to think."

"Well then, don't try to think; leave it at that," I answered encouragingly, afraid lest he might remember Miss St. Chair and begin to ask inconvenient questions. "You have not got to worry about anything at present, the doctors say. until you are better: and now I'm going to leave you, if you will promise not to trouble about anything. Mr. Clymping will come to see you any time the doctors allow him, he is very pleased to have you here: and Colonel Gorleston has been down and will come down again soon."

I could see that anything more at the moment would be too much for him; so, nodding to the nurse, I left him with a reassuring pressure of the hand.

Then I went downstairs and told Burgess and Ann exactly how he was: and, with Burgesses permission, I telephoned Major Blenkinsopp at Scotland Yard and advised him exactly how things stood, and that, so far. Lord Bullingdon remembered nothing that could assist—in. fact, that his memory was a blank upon the whole subject.

After that he went on famously, the subject of the accident being studiously avoided, and no reference being made to anything that might disturb him. Burgess and Ann were both allowed to see him; and the latter, to her delight, was permitted to take her share of sitting with and reading to him. Colonel Gorleston ran down again with Sir Humphrey Bedell on the Sunday: and he was promised in due course that he should see Bellingham and Verjoyce. To Miss St. Clair he made no reference. Possibly she had temporarily been banished from his mind in connexion with the accident by the shock; or he was waiting to ask them about her.

XIII

Meanwhile my one outstanding anxiety for the moment, which was holding up my plans, was the fact that I had had no cable from Mauders as to his return: and it was an intense relief to me to find one waiting when we came in from a morning walk over the down on Monday. It was sent from Vienna and said:

"No doubt about John. Back Thursday. Meet me midday Temple.

—MANDERS."

I felt a clutch at my heart. It spelt the climax of the great drama, which was so swiftly drawing to a head. unless I were mistaken. Yet withal it was an immense relief: and, self-reliant as I am both by nature and as the result of circumstance, I do not mind admitting that I was glad to feel that I should soon have his quick, alert brain with its full appreciation of the case. To say nothing of his strong personality, beside me to help as the crisis approached. Moreover, it meant that I should at last be able to take Burgess into my full confidence; and, whatever the cost to himself, I knew that I would then have another strong resolute collaborator To rely upon, in addition to being at last in a position to clear up all reservation between us. The latter. I own. was perhaps a little selfish, but few people will ever realize what it had meant to me to live with him hour by hour as his guest and his oldest friend under such circumstances. Facts had to be faced: and I knew from my long acquaintance with his character that he was a man who would rather face things than burke them.

"Manders will he back on Thursday morning," I said, putting the cable into my pocket; "and I shall have to run up to town. His mission, apparently, has been successful from the point of view I anticipated; and upon my return. Burge, old friend, I shall be able to explain everything and clear up this beastly mystery between us; though God knows you will like it even less than I do."

Burgess nodded.

"I am content, as I trust I have shown, to leave myself in your hands," he said quietly.

"Whatever is right or for the best you may rely upon me to do."

"I know that," I said with emphasis, as Ann called us to come to lunch.

Dorothy came and spent the afternoon, and I must confess I liked her more than ever. But she struck me as looking pale and worried: and I had my fears as to the old man. Of him I had seen enough for my purpose; and I had no desire to further the acquaintance, however great his genius or however valuable his scientific knowledge. He was, to my mind. an object lesson in the value of life's simplicities, the real things that make for happiness after all. Further, I had no desire unnecessarily to visit the decaying atmosphere of the Dower House.

And so what between Bullingdon's progress, visits of doctors with good reports, and other folk, including Blenkinsopp, and general trivialities. The next Two days passed without incident,

Ann was full of her patient; and we saw Dorothy again on the Wednesday, pale but red-lipped, and—possibly my imagination—it seemed to me that her eyes were contracting and lengthening towards the ends of the lids- a strange phenomenon.

But of the Professor we saw nothing; and Dorothy informed us that he had one of his high pressure working fits on, and would brook no interruption for meals or anything else.

XIV

On the eve of Manders' return the moon entered its first quarter; and somehow I was hardly astonished to hear. upon my way to the station to catch the 9.30, that two more sheep had been found mutilated on the downs a little farther south than before. It all coincided; and I should have been surprised, rather than otherwise; had any attempt been made to devour the carcases.

Still, it added yet one more to the many things I had to think about going up in the trains and from Victoria I drove straight to my solicitor's to get from him the statement I had left in his hands, as it was my intention to take it in person to Scotland Yard that afternoon, accompanied by Manders, when we had talked everything out finally.

I was at Garden Court on the stroke of noon and found him there, bathed and shaved after his journey, and none the worse for his long trip, though I fancied that there was a slightly wonted expression in his eyes.

However, he greeted me cheerfully enough, as we gripped hands, speaking in a light tone which was in reality far removed from both of us.

"Phew," he said, passing me a cigar', "there is not a possible shadow of doubt in my mind as to your being only too correct in your surmises about our friend 'John.' In Berlin I could get nothing beyond praise of his scientific work—of his personality little or nothing. All was vague; but it was obviously a subject which no one seemed inclined to pursue. He has not actually resided in Berlin for over twenty-five year's. So on I went to Vienna. There again I was baffled—- everything equally vague and unsatisfactory. There too. he has not actually resided for a very long time; and his visits of recent years have been intermittent and never prolonged. In one instance—that of Professor Mendel, to whom you luckily gave me a letter—I received some pretty strong hints of something very wrong, confirming your' suspicions; and he practically said that, whatever it was, he was a man of baleful influence, and that no one who knew anything of him would have anything to do with him. Better still—obviously not wishing to be more explicit himself—he gave me one or two clues, which took me to the Harz Mountains and then on into Rumania. As you can imagine. I had not much time: and without Professor Mendel's hints and names of places I could never have done what I have in these few days. I found out that he was never very long in one place at a time, leading a strange recluse's life, and always leaving a trail behind him of strange, unaccountable disappearances. There were weird tales that the peasants would hardly breathe; but I found one or two in different places, mostly older people, who spoke out their suspicions quite frankly. His final departure is completely wrapped in mystery; and no one I saw or spoke to seemed to have the least idea as to whither he had vanished or where he was. Here," he concluded, handing me a bundle of manuscript, "are the details all collated, ready for immediate use. I think that they will be found pretty convincing—certainly so far as we ourselves are concerned."

"You have done wonders in the time," I said, taking the manuscript; "and I am most grateful for your help. It has come just at the critical moment, and will, I trust, be the means of convincing the authorities and saving something possibly worse, at an early date, even than what has already happened—if, indeed, that be possible."

And I told him my fears with regard to Dorothy; and his face grew very grave.

"My God," he said in a low tone, "that is too horrible to think of, especially with your' friend Clymping head over ears in love with the girl in his solid, complete fashion, and Walpurgis Nacht next Tuesday. We haven't a moment to waste."

"No," I agreed. "Just let me study this document of yours, while you study this one of mine, which I drew up after you left. Then this afternoon we must get right through to headquarters at the Yard, and thrash the whole thing out— and, what is more, convince them at any cost."

I read Manders' statement through carefully twice, and. though naturally somewhat vague and elusive in itself, it was quite convincing enough when added to the other facts we had to work upon. dovetailing into the whole and making one complete piece—that is. if anything could ever convince the official British mind of things that stand outside the ordinary courses of nature in these latter days. I was especially struck by these events surrounding the Professor's final disappearance from Transylvania, when his life was actually in danger amongst the superstitious peasants. But were they so superstitious after all; or rather were they not in closer touch with elemental facts than we of the West? The Brighton Road mysteries were only history repeating itself after all—at no very distant interval.

"The two statements piece Together admirably," said Manders, giving counsel's opinion, as he laid down my manuscript: "and you have covered the case from this end most concisely and completely. You have a legal mind, while fortunately lacking the verbosity of the law,"

The compliment I must admit pleased me, coming from such a source.

Then for nearly an hour we went over everything in considerable detail, cross-questioning each other upon the statements, and getting things finally into order for official presentation; and I laid before Manders the plan of action which I had sketched out in my own mind.

"Drastic, but practical and to the point," was his only comment. "Personally I approve; but what if the authorities do not?"

"Then," I answered, looking him straight in the eyes. "I shall take the law into my own hands—that is- if human law there be in such a case standing outside all human laws. Burgess Clymping, I know, will not fail me.'"

Fitzroy Manders laughed in his light way, which often disguised so much beneath the crust.

"I shall be in at The finish, too, old chap," he said, "don't you fret. I don't believe in leaving a job half done. I like seeing things through myself."

"But your career, your future?" I said. "Suppose anything should be wrong? We are on very dangerous ground in event of failure, or even a serious hitch."

Manders laughed again.

"With our facts and you in command we will so organize things that there.will be no failure," he said with quiet assurance.

Then he looked at his watch.

"By George, five minutes to two! You will be hungry after your early breakfast: I was a bit late myself. I'll ring up Scotland Yard and get an appointment for this afternoon; and then we will go off to the Garrick and have lunch."

He rang up himself his clerk being out, and got through to Major Blenkinsopp's room, only to find that he was at lunch and not expected back till three o'clock; so he left word that he would telephone at that time for an appointment, adding that it was most urgent.

We lunched in a quiet comer; and I told Manders everything that had happened during his absence. He was specially interested in my visit to the Professor and my investigation of his habits firsthand; and I found that during his trip he had been studying the literature of these strange elemental things, besides having learnt a good deal about it from The folk-lore of the peasants and some of the tales which had been told him first-hand.

At three o'clock he went to the telephone, and returned in a few minutes with the news that he had arranged an interview with Sir Thomas Brayton at four o'clock, at which Major Blenkinsopp would be present also. We were To go to Blenkinsopp's room at ten minutes to four, and he would take us straight through and introduce me. Manders himself had met the Chief two or three times, although he did not know him well.

We were in Blenkinsopp's room up to time. and he greeted us both most cordially.

"Mauders tells me that you have some very important and extraordinary facts to lay before the Chief with regard to the Brighton Road affairs," he said, as we shook hands; "and I can only say, between ourselves. That we shall be very receptive, we are candidly at our wits' end, and public comment has been none too kind of late."

I frowned slightly, but decided not to prejudice my case by saying that probably—certainly if I had my way—the public would never know the truth; and would continue for all time to blame Scotland Yard as the ever handy scapegoat in all cases of crime either undiscovered; or upon which they are not fully enlightened with all the morbid details which sell the newspapers and spice their breakfast-tables.

"I trust I shall be able to help," I answered; "but, as the matter is a somewhat long and abstruse one; it is no good my starting on it till we are with Sir Thomas Brayton,"

Blenkinsopp nodded acquiescence, and asked Lord Bullingdon and the news from Clymping.

"And that surly old brute of a German professor?" he added.

"We are coming To him," I replied, a trifle grimly: and he shot a quick glance across at me. He seemed as Though he were about to speak, but checked himself.

XV

Sir Thomas Brayton received us cordially and motioned us to sit down. He was seated at a big table looking out across the rivers and I purposely took a chair opposite to him, with Manders supporting me on my right, laying our two statements on the table for reference.

"You have some special information with regard to the Brighton Road business which you wish to lay before me personally; Mr. Osgood," he said without beating about the bush and I saw That it was up to me to make good.

I first explained my position in the matter, and how, through Burgess Clymping, I had, so to speak, been pitchforked right into the middle of the affair at its height upon my arrival in England three weeks before; and then I added a short explanation with regard to Manders. and how he had come into the business equally unexpectedly.

Sir Thomas nodded.

"Mr. Manders is known to me personally; and. his considered opinion, in all matters like this, carries great weight."

It encouraged me, and gave me confidence to feel that I was introduced under such good auspices, considering the strangeness of the story which I was about to put forward.

"Then, as his opinion fully coincides with mine. Sir Thomas," I said with slight emphasis, "I trust that you will not too readily write me down a freak or a lunatic, but hear me through in detail, and with an open mind go into these two statements, which I have brought for your perusal and that of Major Blenkinsopp—one by Mr. Manders and the other by myself—dealing with the case from two points of view."

The Chief made a slightly impatient gesture.

"You may rest assured on the subject."

"Thank you," I said: and then I leant forward a trifle across the table.

"Have you ever studied the subject of lycanthropy?" I asked.

I could swear he started slightly. Again he nodded, as much as to convey that he knew something about the subject theoretically or academically, but that it was not one that he had ever entertained seriously in the sphere of practical everyday life or modem crime, especially in Twentieth-century England.

"Professor Lycurgus Wolff and his old servant. Anna Brunnolf are werewolves," I said, solemnly; "and they are responsible for the disappearances on the Brighton Road."

I heard Blenkinsopp breathe deeply. The sound of a man deeply moved.

The Chief tapped his blotting-pad with a big blue pencil, looking across at me noncommittally.

"Go on," he said without comment and for an instant I wondered if either or both were doubting my sanity—I, a strange American in London, advancing a theory so bizarre as to astound even the heads of Scotland Yard!

"The lore of lycanthropy and the manifold legends of werewolves are one of The oldest things in the world, and appear in practically every country in Europe and Asia, including such outlying places as Iceland, Lapland, and Finland. To say nothing of other Continents, including even my own country: and it would hardly seem logical, upon the face of it. that there should be no foundation in fact for such widely spread—aye, and widely behoved stories, many bearing close examination.

"In The fifteenth century a council of theologians was actually convoked upon the subject by the Emperor Sigismund; and they solemnly decided in convocation that the werewolf was a reality. Amongst the ancients—without going into the matter deeply at the moment—Herodotus describes the Neuri as persons who had the power of assuming the shape of wolves once a year. Pliny relates that one of The family of Antæus was each year chosen by lot to be transformed into a wolf. Ovid, as doubtless you will recall, tells how Lycäon, King of Arcadia, was turned into a wolf for testing The divinity of Jove by serving up to him a 'hash of human flesh.' Again St. Patrick in more recent times converted Vereticus, King of Wales- into a wolf. And so on ... without labouring legends and piling up detail, though, in passing, I may add, perhaps not without point, the fact that in Great Britain itself in the North, in The history of the County of Durham, the actual name 'Bnunolf itself is on record, and Gervase, of Tilbury, in his Otia Imperiala.' writes: 'Vidimus enim frequenter in Anglia per lunationes homines in lupos mutari, quod homimun genus

gerulphos Galli nominant, Angli vero "were-wulf " dicunt'
Finally, surely the most primitive and obvious werewolf
legend of all. accepted from the earliest days of our
dawning intelligence, is the tale of 'Little Red Riding
Hood'?

"In the whole history of demonology—the superphysical, spiritual projection, elementals, and so forth—
which- as the result of civilization has been growing less
and less, or been more concealed where such things still
flourish in isolated or, at worst, sporadic fashion—things
which, by the aid of science and the development of
modern thought, we are again beginning to reconsider and
reclass in many instances in the light of greater
knowledge—in the whole of this world-long and world-
wide history there is an unbroken sequence which cannot
but carry conviction of itself. As a modem writer phrases it
with regard to those other elementals, vampires—These
intangible beings, who, though scoffed at in an age of
materialism and negation, have throughout history given
intermittent evidences of their existence... who belong to
that unseen world to whose mystic manifestations time
imaginative and soul-seers of all times have testified.' It is
very well put and applies equally to werewolves. who are
super-physical hybrids of the material and the immaterial:
and their power of metamorphosis dates back as far as can
be traced, growing less and less frequent, as I have said,
with the advance of civilization and the better ordering of
things. However, this is not the side of the matter which I
wish to labour. Doubtless you are familiar with it in the
main"—Sir Thomas shook his head a trifle irritably—"and
I have embodied the essentials in this statement of mine
with references to the literature of the subject in many
languages."

I paused and drew breath,

"It was a subject that at one period was equally academic to my mind, though fascinating, I must admit, from the first time I struck it in my reading: but I have, as a man of means and leisure, ever since I left school, made travel my hobby, and I have been amazed at the legendry I have come across first-hand in all soils of isolated parts—in the Harz Mountains, Austria-Hungary, the Balkans. The Caucasus, Russia, Siberia—and. more than that. modern cases of lycanthropy firmly believed in and vouched for locally. I have had actual werewolf men and women pointed out to me—families of werewolves who have a lycanthropic inheritance of many generations; and it is years since, as the result of actual personal investigation, that I have accepted lycanthropy as a fact—rare. but perhaps not so rare as people in circumscribed London imagine. It is essentially a survival, so far as it does survive, on the outer fringes, driven into outlying and outlandish places, and segregated by civilization and the rough-and ready methods of centuries towards those convicted or often only suspected of lycanthropy. It is centuries since there was a case—at least, an actually authenticated case—of lycanthropy in Great Britain, though there have been strange stories touching upon it even in more recent times and certain unexplained manifestations, again in outlying and isolated parts. But the werewolf in this country and in Ireland is a fact as well established as in any other, if not so frequent in instance. I can give you specific references, but again I do not wish to labour this part of my statement unduly with quotations from Bodleian MSS., Richard Verstegen in his 'Restitution of Decayed Intelligence' in 1605. and the like. Why, the very story of the dog Gelert is a werewolf legend in itself! But in the present case in hand we have not to fall back upon British lycanthropic lore itself for justification or substantiation, as here it is plainly a matter of importation." Again I paused.

XVI

Blenkinsopp was staring hard at me, so hard that he
scarcely seemed to see me in his absorbed intentness. The
weirdness of it was gripping him. I could see: and once or
twice I had felt as much as seen Manders nod
encouragingly. But so far I had evoked no encouragement
from the Chief.

"And to apply your theory?" he said, raising his eyebrows
a trifle, and drumming away more vigorously than ever
with his infernal blue pencil on his pad.

"I was as much at a loss as anybody to start with, to be
candid," I continued; "no clue, nothing seemingly to get
hold of. Yet the key to the whole tiring I felt instinctively
lay in Lord Bullingdon's oft reiterated delirium—obviously
the last impression upon his conscious mind, and that a
sharp and sudden one—'Big dog . . . jumped over moon . . .
green eyes.' I repeated it over and over again to myself. It
ran through my brain day and night. I could neither get rid
of it nor hit upon its significance. Its very absurdity,
suggestive of a nursery rhyme, seemed to me to accentuate
its importance, and to take it out of the sphere of the events
of everyday grown-up life—a paradox perhaps, but none
the less a fact in such matters of deduction. And so it
thrummed and hammered away insistently in my head, till
the next light was supplied by the visit of this Professor
Lycurgus Wolff himself, who interested me intellectually
as much as he repulsed me physically, setting something
working subconsciously at the back of my brain. Then, that
evening, when I was sitting smoking and puzzling, it came
to me in a flash. The Professor was an absolutely typical
example of a werewolf in its human shape that one could
well imagine, with his remarkably bright piercing black
eyes under the characteristic long slanting brows, meeting
in a point over his nose—his pointed ears set low and far

back on his head—his brilliantly white, strong teeth, almost like fangs—his full mouth, with its bright red lips—his long pointed hands with their curiously projecting third fingers and their red, almond-shaped curving nails—his general hairiness of aspect—his stoop—and, above all, his peculiar long swinging stride, which is, perhaps, the most characteristic of the lot, to which must be added his habit of wearing and his predilection for fur. Had it not been that in such an environment of all places, I was as little ready or likely to suspect any possibility of lycanthropy as either you or Major Blenkinsopp or my friend Manders here; it would have come to me more easily: but we are not on the look-out for such things in Sussex. When it did come. however, it seemed to strike me full between the eyes, almost dazing me."

I saw that Sir Thomas was showing a little more interest, and that his pencil was quiet for a moment.

"So," I continued, "as I have put down in detail in my statement, I reviewed the whole situation from his unexpected appearance in the wood, when Miss Clymping was luckily guarding Lord Bullingdon. and his destroyal of certain clues which annoyed Major Blenkinsopp so much at the time, the laceration of Lord Bullingdon's shoulder, and so forth. I knew that at that point it would be futile to advance my theory officially; so, by a lucky inspiration, I determined to enlist the assistance of Mr. Manders to go abroad and investigate the private history of this famous German scientist, while I, at home, looked into his habits and mode of life. Mr. Manders only returned this morning; and his statement, more than bears out all my anticipations. He has put it. into writmg; and I will read it to you."

I did so, ending with the climax of Wolffs hurried and secret flight from Transylvania to escape what we call lynching—a story practically bringing home to him any allegations or accusations I might make, a ghastly tale of children and young girls, in the main, disappearing with increasing frequency until it became a case of almost nightly—Totally without clue, as in the Brighton Road business. At last suspicion began to fix itself upon Professor Wolff and Anna Brunnolf and the word "werewolf began to take shape in the minds and on the lips of the peasantry, until they commenced to grow threatening—and then suddenly, without warning or trace. The Professor and his old maidservant disappeared. These events had happened some two years ago: and there were slight references in the papers at the time—not, of course, to the Professor, but to the mysterious series of disappearances in Transylvania.

Sir Thomas nodded a quick assent, showing that he had some recollection of the matter; and I felt that I had scored a strong point at last,

Then I took up my own end of the story in Sussex.

"In and round that now tainted old Dower House, gentlemen," I said solemnly, "I saw and smelt enough to convince the most cynical of sceptics. Never did a place in so short a time reek more of lycanthropy and all its filthy surroundings—the typical smell of decay and strange pungent odour, indescribable yet animal."

And I recapitulated all the seemingly trivial facts that I have set down at some length in this document, not only with regard to the Professor and his ways. his habit of devouring quantities of raw meat, his obsession of fur, and other characteristic matters, but laying special stress upon the strange pools of water, which are typically lycanthropous, and the hideous yellow flowers with then black protuberances, together with the white and red ones, all reeking of lycanthropy and; worse still, capable of communicating it and contaminating those coming into contact with these two recognized sources of impregnation—in many ways the most diabolical part of the whole affair, to my mind, with its obvious intention of founding a cult of lycanthropy in the very heart of England itself, which, if not realized and frustrated, might take years to eradicate, or possibly never be eradicated at all.

Then—a small point perhaps, but a very convincing one to Those who trust animal instinct as I do, especially in the case of a dog—there was Whiskers' deadly fear and horror, not only of the pools themselves, but of the old house under its changed conditions, and the way in which he would not enter it even with his master, and his equal fear and avoidance of the Professor, from whom he always slunk: away with his hair raised and his tail between his legs.

Finally, There was the climax of the sheep on the downs, which I pointed out was a very typical instance of "werewolf mischief, when he kills out of malign freakishness, or for sheer lust of killing, and not for food, lacerating and disembowelling and leaving his victims to die, and I also drew particular attention to the influence of the moon upon such mauifestations.

"And this. sir," I went on. drawing to a conclusion, "brings me to a point that is both vital and immediate. The moon always has a most marked and malign occult influence upon all elementals, a point too well recognized for it to be necessary for me to dilate upon or to labour it; and in this case it has been most marked. The Bolsover tragedy occurred about midnight at full moon on February 2, you will remember. The Bullingdon St. Chair affair at full moon on Sunday, April 1. also about midnight, the hour which has special influences upon elementals and evil spirits.

"Next Tuesday," I went on solemnly and impressively,, "is not only full moon, but it is Walpurgis Nacht, a most sinister coincidence: and in the present case, especially when preceded by these two minor affairs of the sheep on the downs, showing elemental restlessness and a blood-craving, it is practically bound, in my judgment, to lead up to a horrible climax, an orgy of some diabolical character which will put the other tragedies into the shade. Walpurgis Nacht is the night of the year which makes the initiated shudder. It is the night when all evil spirits and elementals are released to hold Hell's own high festival and practise every orgy of vice; when human sacrifice, above all, is ever at its height. On that night the peasants of the Near East, in isolated parts, retire to their homes before sunset, and nothing will induce them to venture forth for fear of what may happen to them, such is their firm belief in these super-physicals and elementals of all sorts. It is the great night of All Evil, and they lie huddled close in their beds and cross themselves and I ask you, therefore. whether a full moon at midnight synchronizing with Walpurgis Nacht, cannot but be an irresistible combination in malign influence, especially with the signs of activity we have already seen with the new moon and in its first quarter? Frankly I feel convinced in my own mind and fear the worst, if we do not act and take effective precautions to rid. not merely Sussex and the Brighton Road, but Great Britain itself of this horrible importation of incarnate evil."

Blenkinsopp was breathing deeply and had not moved, like a man fascinated: and Sir Thomas had stopped tapping his pad and was leaning forward slightly, his eyes fixed intently on my face. Manders was nodding from time to time in his characteristic fashion.

"The Professor, wolf by name as by nature, and Anna Brunnolf are werewolves," I reiterated with strong emphasis, "undoubtedly and beyond all question werewolves, hybrid beasts of prey, such as in these days we have no organized or recognized way of dealing with. They will, I am fully convinced, metamorphose on Tuesday night and wreak havoc, exacting human toll. Of the daughter, Dorothy—or Dorothea, as the old man prefers to call her—

I am hopeful, but unceitain. It does not seem to me that she has shown any signs of inherited lycanthropy up to the present, and I am morally certain that she has never suffered metamorphosis; or why should her father be so obviously trying to impregnate her by the recognized means—especially those thrice-damnable flowers? There are symptoms, however, that she is tending that way—the increasing redness of her lips and her finger-nails to that peculiar vivid tint. Her eyes, too, show signs. Then there are two other noticeable points—onc ncgativc and thc othcr positive—her growing lack of enjoyment of sweet things and her increasing liking for raw meat diet. My fear and my anticipation is that this may all be heading up to that irresistible combination on Walpurgis Nacht, and that next Tuesday night may be the fatal hour other first metamorphosis against her will and even her own consciousness. To my mind it adds a very grave aspect to this whole terrible business."

I stopped and sat back, keeping my eyes on the Chief.

XVII

"And what steps do you propose to take?" he asked, speaking non-committally still and calmly enough, but with a touch of suppressed excitement in his voice. "I presume that you have a plan in your mind?"

"Yes, I have, sir," I replied promptly and emphatically. "I propose, with the help of certain good friends, and possibly with your official assistance, to picket the Dower House on Tuesday night and to shoot down any werewolf or werewolves that may show themselves."

The Chief raised his eyebrows.

"I shall have at least half a dozen crack shots posted, three at the front and three at the back, armed with Winchester repeaters. The night should be almost as light as day, and the visibility good; and there should be no mistake. If no werewolves appear, there will be no shooting; but a very careful watch would then have to be preserved over the house till things prove themselves one way or the other."

Again the Chief was drumming upon his pad with his blue pencil, beating a regular tattoo.

"And how do you promise to dispose of your werewolves and account for the disappearance of their human counterparts?" he asked dryly.

I leant forward again over the table, focusing my eyes hard on him: and in a few words I detailed my further plan for covering all tracks, adding certain reasons connected with the exigencies of lycanthropy.

"By God, Mr. Osgood," he said quietly, in a tone I took to be quite complimentary, "I must say that you are a cool hand. In fact, you would make a fine criminal. It is a pity you have missed your vocation, as you would have given us some stirring times in the sleepy old C.I.D. And pray what do you propose to do if I do not see eye to eye with you— and Mr. Manders; I presume?" Manders nodded quick cordial assent—"and refuse my consent, to such unorthodox action?"

I looked him straight in the face.

"Then, God helping me, sir, I shall take matters into my own hands and act without it, and stand or fall by what happens."

"And I, too," broke in Manders incisively. The Chief laughed.

"I am much obliged to you, gentlemen, for all your trouble in This most extraordinary affair," he said. rising and holding out his hand to each of us in turn. "Leave your documents with Major Blenkinsopp and myself; and be good enough, if you will, to call upon me to-morrow morning at ten-thirty."

Blenkinsopp shook hands most warmly; and I could see that he, at least, had been convinced.

XVIII

That night I spent at Manders' house, and we sat late into The night thrashing out the details of the plan of action until we had them all cut and dried.

The next morning, needless to say, we were at Scotland Yard in good time. and went straight to Blenkinsopp's room.

He greeted us cordially.

"You have won through with the Chief" he said.

"At first he was incredulous to a degree, and regarded the whole business as preposterous, as a wild and utterly impossible theory; but he was coming round before you left. He and I were up nearly all night reading and discussing your documents; and I don't mind telling you that we consulted certain authorities upon lycanthropy. Now come along," he concluded, looking at the clock, "as the Chief hates to be kept waiting."

Sir Thomas Brayton greeted us both less officially and with more cordiality; and then. after we were seated, he put us through a very vigorous and searching cross-examination, covering the whole ground—past. present, and future.

At the end of two hours he gave his decision.

"Well; gentlemen," he said, "it is a strange proceeding and entirely unorthodox: but unorthodox cases demand unorthodox methods at times. You may shoot any wolf or any number of wolves you may see anywhere in Sussex— there is neither legal nor moral harm in that. But, mind you," he added impressively, "if there be any taking of human life, you will do it at your own risk, and will be held responsible."

He paused and looked at us almost sternly.

"I will take all responsibility," I said, "and stand or fall by what happens."

"And I, too," again said Manders. with sharp decision.

"Then I will send down a high confidential official with special instructions and full powers to act" said the Chief "as a safeguard both to yourselves and ourselves."

Then Blenkinsopp spoke.

"With your permission, sir, I will go myself."

The Chief nodded: and so it was arranged to my intense relief and satisfaction, as time was growing perilously short.

Part III

THE DOWER HOUSE IN THE HOLLOW

Thus, to my intense relief, it was arranged that Major Blenkinsopp should accompany us back to Clymping Manor in a semi-official capacity; and it was a proof that Scotland Yard did not regard me as a hopeless lunatic or a weaver of wild fantasies. Had it turned out otherwise. I had had the fullest intention of acting upon my own responsibility and taking the risk, so convinced was I that I was right, and that this grave danger not only to sleepy Sussex, but to Great Britain in general, must be extirpated at all costs. Under such circumstances, however, there would at the least have been the fullest inquiries and much unpleasant publicity throughout the length and breadth of the world, if no worse consequences, whereas now I was hopeful that, skilfully managed, it might be hushed up by official consent in the public interest—a thing by no means unknown in certain cases.

We went with Blenkinsopp back to his room. where he had ordered lunch—cold chicken and ham, followed by bread and cheese, with beer in tankards.

"Rough and ready," he said. "but it saves time. I have to be back with the Chief at two, which doesn't leave too much time. I knew that I could neither take you fellows out to lunch nor go out with you; so I thought we had better lunch here. You can have whisky and soda, if you prefer it, it's in me cupboard."

"Beer for me," said Manders in his usual cheerful way, which was worth its weight in radium at times of crises. "A meal for the gods; and I'm jolly hungry after being in the witness-box so long. Change of air induces appetite, I wonder if my little efforts always make my victims equally voracious, if not veracious?

And he laughed a trifle ironically as we sat down. "I can't guarantee getting away before four o'clock, if so early." said Blenkinsopp, "as. when I have done with the Chief, I have one or two important things to fix up here and hand over to somebody else for the best part of a week or so, as I'm determined to make Clymping Manor my headquarters, with its owner's kind permission, till we've seen this ugly business through."

"So am I." said Manders. "Osgood here can telephone after lunch and tell Clymping that we are both inviting ourselves down for a week in the country, even if we should chance to run up to town for a few hours, if we get bored. My wife's away up north with her sister; and I'll wire her to stay on for a few days. I'll drive you both down in the car this afternoon, calling here for you, Blenkinsopp, at four; and, if you are busy, we will wait in the Black Museum, if Osgood hasn't seen it. How will that suit?"

"Splendid." said I, greatly heartened; "and I know Burgess will not only be delighted, but devoutly grateful to you both, especially when he learns the whole truth. Moreover, God knows I shall be glad beyond all telling to have you two by me, when I have to enlighten him and convince him of the strange truth. It will be an awful blow to him, especially as far as it touches poor Dorothy Wolff."

They both nodded gravely; and it brought us back to the matter in hand and the grim reality of things.

"It complicates a beastly job by bringing in the personal element a bit too acutely," said Manders grimly: "but, by gad, we've got to see it through and lay old Pere Garou by the heels at all costs, together with his unpleasant old Anna. Please God, there is still some hope for the girl."

"Amen," we both said fervently, praying more and truly from the bottom of our hearts than we had done for many long years, reverting unconsciously to the training and instincts of early youth in the hour of stress, with an absolute lack of self-consciousness; which makes men in the ordinaiy way disguise their deepest feelings with a quip or a veneer of cynicism.

"More cheese?" asked Blenkinsopp, pushing the plate towards me and relieving the situation. "No? All right then. Off you two get as soon as ever you like, and be back at four sharp. I will do my best to be through by then."

We took our dismissal with a laugh and rose from our seats.

"Right-oh," said Manders, resuming his usual cheery tone. "We'll be here in good time."

We took a taxi to the club, where Manders 'phoned Pycombe, telling him to bring the car round at a quarter to four with his kit, and telegraphed to his wife; while I trunk-called Burgess, advising him of our arrival between half-past five and six. He was delighted to hear that I was bringing Manders and Blenkinsopp for the week-end; and I promised to explain everything fully upon our arrival. It was characteristic of him that he asked no questions, but took the situation for granted.

"I'll tell Ann to have their rooms ready," was all he said; and I knew that he, like myself, was at heart more than thankful that we should have two such sound coadjutors by our side in the hour of climax, which, though ignorant of its actual character, he knew to be heading up according to our expectations.

The impeccable Pycombe was inevitably punctual, driving the car himself, though not in uniform; and he was obviously disappointed when Manders took the wheel from him and told him that he should not want him.

"The fewer on the spot. me better," he said to me as we drove down Whitehall, "outside the actual actors in the forthcoming Drury Lane drama in real life: and I can always send for him if I want him. I can guarantee him as secret as the grave: but he can't shoot." I nodded.

"I've got my shooting squad made up in my mind." I answered, "subject, of course, to Burgess's approval and that of Blenkinsopp and yourself. I want it to be a strictly amateur team as far as possible."

Blenkinsopp did not keep us waiting more than five minutes. He was followed by a plain clothes officer with his bag.

"Chief Inspector Boodle," he explained, "my right-hand confidential man, who may prove invaluable. I shall tell him everything in due course: but at the house he will simply appear amongst the servants as my valet,"

We were a silent party on the way down, Blenkinsopp sitting in front beside Manders, while I sat in me back with Boodle and the kit-bags, deep in thought. We all felt that at length we were really launched upon our grim hazard for better, for worse, playing for higher stakes than we had ever dreamt of—human lives, perhaps our own. and at least one human soul.

In Redhill an "A.A." scout took our number and warned us of police-traps, and Blenkinsopp thanked him with ironic effusiveness: and beyond that point I noticed, with interest, that the road was well patrolled by police, both mounted and on foot. The scout was right, and twice we found ourselves in traps; but Blenkinsopp's badge, when shown, produced a complete change of front from aggressiveness to apology.

Mutton was awaiting us in Crawley, as instructed by telephone by Blenkinsopp, who advised him that he had come down to take charge until further notice, though the fact was to be kept a profound secret, and that he would be installed at Clymping Manor as headquarters. Mutton was to call there for orders either from Blenkinsopp or in his absence, from Boodle, and keep in touch by telephone. It saved Mutton's face locally and with the wider public; and, at the same time, it suited Blenkinsopp's book to leave him ostensibly in charge.

"I shall have to use poor Mutton as a blind," he said, with a little laugh, as we started off afresh; "but I can make it up to him later, as it is really not his fault, after all, that he has not got to the bottom of this business."

Burgess greeted us all warmly, and Boodle, playing his part, was handed over to Jevons, while we greeted Ann in the hall and settled down to tea and buttered toast.

"Chocolates," I said, after she had kissed me, "for a good little girl, or, rather, a buxom young nurse."

Shut up, Line," she said, laughing. "You'll make me bilious and unfit me for my arduous duties."

"And how is your patient?" I inquired.

"He is doing splendidly." she answered; "and to-morrow Sir Harry Verjoyce and Mr. Wellingham are coming down to lunch, and are to be allowed to see him for a few minutes. He seems worried about something, and has been begging to be allowed to see them; so Sir Humphrey thought it better that he should see one, if not both."

"Well, don't worry him with any news of our arrival. Miss Clymping said Blenkinsopp, passing his cup for more tea. "It can serve no good purpose at the moment, and might worry him. The less he ever remembers of this ghastly business, the better for him in the future. From what I learn from inquiries in town, I don't fancy that his affair with Miss St. Clair' was quite so serious as the romantic or the purient public tried to persuade itself; and it was certainly on the wane, as both Verjoyce and Wellingham will, I am sure confirm. She was quite a good girl and the best of company, but now that she is, I fear. beyond recall, it can do nobody any good to rake up the harrowing details, especially in the case of an invalid who has had such a severe shock both mentally and physically"

I noticed a queer little look, as though of relief, pass over Ann's pretty face; and I chimed in to save her from answering.

"Yes. I quite agree with Major Blenkinsopp-" I said; "and, Ann dear. you must try to let that part of the matter rest yourself. It does not concern you, and you can do no good: and I hate to think of you mixed up in these horrors. I know you are wonderfully capable for your age, but you are too young: and it is quite outside your sphere."

"I'm with you both." broke in Burgess in his serious way, taking her hand in his almost fatherly fashion. "You stick to the nursing, dear, and leave the rest to us."

Ann nodded in her funny little way. "Yes, I suppose it is best." she said. with a touch of reluctance. "I'll try to do what you all advise. I do try never to think of the horror of the whole thing."

And then I changed me subject, and began telling her about our being police-trapped and the constables' faces when they saw Blenkinsopp's special badge.

"Your Sussex and Surrey police are the limit," I said, laughing: "and there is old Burge, who sits on the local bench once a week and doles out heavy fines upon the poor unfortunate mice who are trapped, while he himself never dreams of keeping within the limit."

"No, he doesn't," said Ann, taking up the cudgels on behalf of her adored big brute; "he always protests solemnly and dissents from—well, I mustn't mention names, or he will be angry with me; and give me a little lecture upon youth and indiscretion when he gets me alone."

"You're a saucy little minx, my dear Ann," I said solemnly, "and could do with a good spanking at times as well as a mere lecture. Your brother is too fond and gentle to you. Now if I were your brother..."

"Thank heaven you're not," interrupted Ann, making her eleven-year-old face at me. "If you were, I'd run away or do something awful! Have a chocolate, Mr. Manders?"

Manders took one. and kept the ball rolling till nn announced that it was time for her to go upstairs and attend to her hospital duties; and it was not far off dressing-time before we were left alone with Burgess.

"Burge. old chap," I said without any beating about the bush, "we have got a lot of very strange things to tell you and lay before you for your judgment; but it is hardly worth while starting before dinner, as it is a pretty long matter, and will take some time to thresh out in detail. So we had better put it off till after dinner. Send Ann to bed early on some excuse or other, as things must be kept from her as far as possible; and then we four can adjourn to the library and get our teeth into it properly. So far I can tell you, strange and horrible as the whole thing is, I— or rather we, Manders and myself—have been successful up to the difficult point of convincing Scotland Yard itself, including the Chief in person; and Blenkinsopp is down here as the result, if not as a coadjutor, at least as an official referee. However, we will make that, and the position as a whole, quite clear to you this evening. Meanwhile, we must be cheerful in front of Ann, and keep her right out of the wretched business ahead. What's wrong with a bronx before dinner? Shall I mix one?"

"Good scheme," said Manders, as Burgess rang the bell for Jevons and the ingredients: and the cocktails filled up the hiatus pleasantly till dressing-time.

II

Outwardly we were a merry enough party at dinner, though Burge was a bit quiet and evidently thinking deeply, but it was not particularly noticeable, as he is naturally inclined to be quiet if there are several people talking nonsense, and Ann could have had no idea that we were all, so to speak, sitting on a dump of high explosives waiting to strike matches—at least, that was the sort of feeling at the back of my mind, as we worked though Ann's excellent, but substantial dinner—her pet theory in life being that man must be well fed to keep him in a good temper. So far it had proved right, as the men who frequented Clymping were in the main young, and had not yet reached the dyspeptic age.

Burgess told me that he had given her the tip to retire at half-past nine and leave us alone to business.

"As I am to be sent off to bed at half-past nine," she announced in her delightfully candid way, when Jevons put the port on the table, "I shall stay with you till then, so that you shall not lose a single minute more than is necessary of my charming company. Besides. I can't go and sit in the drawing-room all alone and talk to myself like a jibbering idiot, can I, Mr. Manders?"

He laughed.

"Not when there is such port as this knocking about," he said. "Port is, I believe, the weak point in the moral armour of the female—that and gin."

"Gin!" exclaimed Ann. making a face. "How horrid!

"Splendid in cocktails." I said. "You ought to have waited downstairs before dinner instead of rushing off precipitately to your pallid patient. It is the one thing I can do—sling a cocktail."

I noticed, with a little start, the colour come into her cheeks when I referred to Bullingdon; and I began to wonder, my thoughts for the first time wandering in a new train.

And so the irony of light, meaningless conversation, as so often in life, but seldom quite so tensely, was kept up to cover the volcano below that might boil over at any moment.

As the clock struck half-past nine Ann rose. "Time all good little girls were in bed," she said, making a little mock curtsey. "Good night, gentlemen: I will leave you to your business."

Burgess held the door open for her, and kissed her as she passed out into the hall. Then he turned round to us.

"Yes, and now to business," he said very gravely. "You can perhaps imagine how painfully anxious I am to hear what you have to tell, and what plans you have evolved to meet the exigencies of the circumstances. Let us go straight into the library."

On the table there were cigars, decanters and glasses, with a couple of syphons in coolers; and Burgess rang the bell. as we seated ourselves.

"We do not want to be interrupted on any account, Jevons," he said, when his man appeared— "that is. unless anything urgent should arise. You can lock up and send everyone off to bed. If the telephone should ring I will answer it myself. We shan't want anything else. Good night, Jevons."

"Good night, sir," said the man, withdrawing and closing the door behind him.

Then Burgess faced round to me almost abruptly, with his under jaw pushed out a bit in a way I know well.

"Now, Line," he said, "let me hear everything. 'I have waited long enough."

"God knows you have. dear old fnend," I answered with no little response and feeling in my voice, taking my seat opposite to him at the far end of the table, with Blenkinsopp on my right and Manders on my left. "I have felt it as acutely as you, I can assure you, and God knows, whatever may happen in these strange times we chance to have fallen upon I shall never forget it or cease to be thankful that it fell to my lot, at the greatest crisis of my life, to have such a white man and such a friend to deal with. Both Manders and Blenkinsopp know everything and appreciate your magnanimity, your big abnegation, as much as I do."

They both nodded, pulling hard at their cigars—some of the big Ramon Allones I had brought Burgess partly as a present, partly as an apology. At times of tenseness and crisis it is always the small and immaterial matters that catch one's eye, as though the mind were seeking to catch at straws of outside relief.

"But there has been, as you may imagine. Burge, old chap," I went on, speaking with a big grip on myself, "a very sound and sufficient reason for it all, in the first place, it was to save you unnecessary personal pain and anxiety while a very lurid and sensational theory was to say the least of it under suspicion: and it would have been unfair to suggest the most terrible possibilities, involving persons you are in a way interested in, without an atom of proof. However. I will not labour the point."

Burgess looked me straight in me face. "Of course, you mean that you consider that Professor Wolff is concerned in these ghastly affairs?" he said, coming straight to the point in his blunt, morally surgical fashion.

I nodded. So did Manders and Blenkinsopp. Again the immaterial and frivolous would obtrude itself upon my tautened mind: and it suggested Chinese mandarins in comic opera.

"Yes." I said, determined not to mince matters in view of what was coming, "and he involves Dorothy."

Burgess flushed, that deeper difference between a man and a woman: and I thought of Ann's blush only a short while before.

It was his turn to nod-curtly.

"Had it only been the Professor," I went on. "I would gladly have risked the improbability of my apparently wild idea with you, my oldest friend but as it involved a whole household, the tenants of your own Dower House. I was diffident, and preferred to risk being misunderstood for a time by the man whose love and opinion I place first of all things in this world—if he should fail me and misunderstand me, which, thank God, he didn't. If he had, it might have brought matters to a head prematurely, which is the worst generalship in the world; and he would have heard, to his own discontent, what God knows I would have given my very soul to keep from him,"

I didn't mean or want to be intense or melodramatic—it is contrary to my whole nature and habit of life—but one must crave indulgence if, for once in a way in one's life-time, the emotional side get the better of one's control, and one's brain race with too open a throttle. We live in an age of mechanical metaphor.

It was a relief when Manders poured himself out some whisky and squirted some soda into it.

"Bear this in mind throughout. Burge," I went on, clearing the ground—"all I say, and we three believe, must be taken as referring actively only to Professor Wolff and old Anna Bnumolf. Where Dorothy comes in we will discuss later: but for the present you must put her, as far' as possible, right apart in your judgment and consideration of things, as I am absolutely convinced that she is as completely ignorant and unsuspicious of what is behind anything that has occurred as you are—or Ann upstairs. She is merely the victim of circumstances and surroundings—a dear delightful growth in the hot-bed of this hell's brood—as innocent as an unborn baby, not even suspicious of evil."

"Thank God," said Burgess with emphasis. "Now I can listen to and hear anything you have to tell me."

And then, without farther preliminaries, I plunged into the heart of things, repeating almost word for word all that I had told Sir Thomas Brayton, unfolding the tale logically in sequence, and marshalling the facts in proof of my theory. When I first mentioned the word "werewolf," I saw utter incredulity written upon Burge's candid face; and I felt that I had been right, and that here was my oldest friend more prepared to regard me as a lunatic at large than anyone else to whom I had so far broached the theory. At the same time. it was only natural, as it was further outside any possibility of his insular ken and habitual unimaginativeness than the receptive mentality of the others: and I had always realized, in my heart, that he would be the hardest of all to convince. He was prosaic by nature, his outlook agricultural, his surroundings bucolic, and his life the epitome of the happy commonplace, which the highly strung and neurotic are so woefully apt to underestimate. What he had ever heard of such phantasmagoria he had probably forgotten years before; and, so far as I was aware, they were certainly never mentioned as serious topics in the Times, the Field, or the Spectator. At the same time. I knew that I could count upon him for a most faithful and uninterrupted hearing; and it put me on my metal.

I was more precise, if possible, in detail and more definite than I had been even at Scotland Yard, keeping my eyes on his dear honest, stolid face, even repeating myself in places, where I felt, if I did not actually see, scepticism; but in the main his face, as in the ordinary way, was a mask, and his jaw obtruded truculently. Once he gave a short, harsh little laugh; and then, instead of feeling the least offended. I realized how deeply he was moved.

And so I plodded though my thankless task incisively, and with no meretricious comment or pleading for conviction, to its ungracious end.

"Never, my dear Burge." I concluded, introducing the human note for the first time, "has a more damnably thankless or unwelcome job been thrust upon an unwilling guest in his happiest surroundings: and I beg you. therefore, to give the matter all the more serious consideration when you realize how much against the grain it all has been and is."

He nodded and lit another cigar.

"I do." was all his comment. His voice was repressed and concentrated; and he had got himself wonderfully in hand. It was what I had hoped for—expected, I may say—for I have a great respect for Burgess's wonderful sanity and balance of character.

Manders poured me out a drink and passed it without a word: and I thanked him. I needed it badly.

"You must give me time to grasp it all." went on Burgess. "My grip of things is not so quick as that of your trained intellects; but I know. Line. that you would never have put this up to me seriously if it had not been devilish serious to you, and you know that I, on my side, have the most complete confidence in you and your judgment."

It was the most grateful and gratifying moment of my life, and—well, I'm a bit reserved, too, but something almost bowled me over for once.

"The old friendship, Burge," I said, lifting my glass: and by the commonplace I saved myself from making an emotional ass of myself.

Then dear old Manders, a champion right-hand man I would recommend confidently to anybody, took up the tale.

"Now, Clymping." he broke in, in his wonderfully convincing manner, which has decided the verdict of many a dozen good men and true in the courts, "it is up to me to confirm in the most cold-blooded fashion every word Lincoln Osgood has said. and to tell the story of my little Æneid and its results, undertaken because I was, in the first instance, convinced by Osgood, who is one of the very few men who can speak of these things with any authority; and. secondly, because it so happened that I had touched the fringe of them myself in the Near East in his company only a few months ago. Furthermore, fate pitchforked me last full moon into the very heart of the whole business, and I felt, and now feel more keenly than ever. a strong moral obligation to do anything in my power to see things through to the end and help to eradicate this anachronistic pest, which has so strangely obtruded itself in the twentieth century into the very heart of my own country. Apart from everything else, I should he criminally lacking in patriotism and a sense of personal responsibility, if I did not. Hence my presence here to-night as your uninvited guest."

"None the less a very welcome one always," said Burgess with his old-fashioned courtesy, so rare in these casual, happy-go-lucky days.

"Thank you." said Manders in acknowledgment: and then he proceeded to detail most carefully and impressively all that he had discovered upon his sudden journey, building up a very convincing case out of the past history of the ill-omened old Professor and Anna Brunnolf. "You will notice." he concluded, "that Miss Wolff does not in any way appear to be under suspicion.

In fact, she is hardly mentioned: and from what I can gather she has not been with her father very much or for very long. It is the one crumb of comfort in the whole ghastly story. As to the other two, I have no more doubt that they are nothing more or less than werewolves than of the fact that I am sitting here: and our duty is plain and obvious. They must be destroyed."

He spoke coolly and incisively: and Burgess started at his last words. His own mind had not so far travelled to the conclusion of things. He was only groping his way through the initial darkness and trying to find light. The tenseness of the present had, up to this point, excluded the claims of the future.

Then Blenkinsopp took his turn, giving the official touch.

"When Osgood and Manders sprung this extraordinary story upon the Chief and myself at the Yard only yesterday, though it now seems centuries ago," he said quietly. "I was as dumbfounded and knocked over mentally as you are now; and it was only natural after all, as, even at headquarters, we are not accustomed to anything quite so weird and startling. Somehow the whole thing gripped and fascinated me from the very start, so much so that it hardly occurred to me to doubt it: but the Chief told me afterwards that he was incredulous to the point of all but being irritated to begin with- and that it was only the fact that Manders here and his work were so well-known to him that kept him from cutting the consultation abruptly short, and writing Osgood down as a polite, if not a dangerous, lunatic."

I could not refrain from smiling.

"It is what I feared all along," I said; "and that is why I walked warily and took every precaution I could against an anticlimax."

Blenkinsopp nodded and went on: "However, I confess that before Osgood was half through his statement he had got him thoroughly interested and into a neutral, non-committal frame of mind. if nothing more. When Manders and he had both had their say—on the lines you have just heard for yourself—he was practically won over, he admitted to me later on, though at first he could hardly bring himself to admit it, even to himself; and we spent all yesterday evening and a large part of last night over the two statements, which be has retained at the Yard for reference, discussing every detail and even turning up a number of books upon the subject, which we had fetched from the British Museum. This morning's cross-exarmnation clinched matters; and that is why I have his permission to be down here in a semiofficial capacity with large discretionary powers."

Burgess had been sitting for some time with his head in his hands; but, when Blenkinsopp had concluded, he looked up. His face was drawn and ghastly white, like a man with a sick soul. It was as though it had penetrated him more deeply, if with more difficulty, than any of us. There was no disbelief—merely horror—written on his face.

"Thank you." he said in an odd, strained voice, "thank you one and all, old friends and new alike. Do not, for God's sake. think that I am in any way ungrateful—only a bit flattened out. It is apt to knock the stuffing out of the toughest of us to hear such a tale in his own house of people not unconnected with him. and of such horrors on his own little estate. I... I..."

There he stopped, as though something had stuck in his throat and the words would not come out, swallowing hard twice.

Manders once more poured out a drink—a good stiff one—and this time passed it to him: and he took a big gulp eagerly, a thing foreign in every way to his habit, "I think I will go out on the terrace for a few minutes and get some air," he said a little huskily, "if you chaps will excuse me. Line, will you come with me?"

III

I rose without a word and opened one of the long windows. It was a glorious spring night, and the moon was shilling white and clear and cold. only a small portion invisible, and on the verge of coming to fullness—a bare four nights before Walpurgis Nacht. Grimly I hooked up at it in the sky. ill-omened and portentous; and I never loved the moon less, loathing it for those subtle undefined qualities that draw out the worst in the elemental world, and affect the spiritual side of humanity so strangely. Lovers may rave about the moon and write odes, little realizing her harsh cynicism and utter lack of human sympathy; but I shall always have an instinctive honor and dislike of that cold white face in the sky, luring on the unsuspecting to the things beyond.

We stepped out on to the terrace and walked right to the far end in silence. Then suddenly Burgess turned and gripped my arm with a force that almost made me wince.

"Line." he asked in a curious strangled voice, "what about Dorothy? For God's sake tell me the worst—or the best."

I turned and faced him, my heart full of pity and a deeper sympathy than I had ever dreamt of. "Poor old man," I said in a quiet voice, "you needn't tell me how things are with you. I have guessed it from the very first time I ever saw you and Dorothy together; and Ann knows it, too. You will have to be brave and face possibilities: but there is hope. and you must not give up hope while it still exists. Of one thing I am certain—that Dorothy has never yet suffered metamorphosis, that so far she is a young girl pure and simple, and has never taken wolf-shape or been any party to these ghastly raids."

"Ah," breathed Burgess deeply, a strange deep breath of relief and anguish combined. "Moreover." I continued, laying my hand on his arm sympathetically, "she shows no signs whatever to my eyes or understanding of inherited lycanthropy. There is some mystery behind the whole thing: but she does not suggest it in any single detail, however trifling, nor does she seem in any way part of the old Professor. She impresses me as being wholly of her mother, not only physically, but by nature. However, there are two types of lycanthropy—inherited and acquired: and what makes me the more sure that she is not lycanthropic by heredity, is that there are obvious signs that Professor

Wolff—and, probably. Anna Brunnolf as well—is clearly trying to impregnate her—not. I fear. without a certain measure of success." Burgess started, and I heard him swear under his breath,

"Steady, old chap," I went on; "it's no good cursing these foul hybrid obscenities. We shall want all our wits to pit against them. if we are to win through and save the dear girl's immortal soul. That is part of the high stakes we are playing for; and we have to face facts frankly. Before God. Burge, I swear that, if it be humanly possible. I will save her for your sake as well as for her own: but I shall want all your help—your coolest and best brains and nerves."

And I explained to him in detail the signs I had seen of the attempts to impregnate the girl, culmmating in the episode of the horrible orange flower with the black pustules and the deadliness of its moral significance—an episode which, up to that moment, had been kept a dead secret between Dorothy and myself, by instinct on her side, by deliberate intent on mine.

Then I went further, detailing the points that were symptomatic of success—the increasing vividness of the red of her lips; the strange narrowing of her eyes: her susceptibility to the influence of fur, her growing fondness of it, and the habit of wearing it almost as a natural thing; and, finally, her increasing distaste for sweet things, and her growing liking, openly confessed, for meat in its raw state—all little things, but horribly suggestive, each in its own significant way, and in combination well nigh conclusive to my mind.

"We cannot say definitely." I concluded judicially, "how far the poison has worked, or how far the damage has been done: but I fear the worst, to be candid. My own idea is that the Professor, in his devilish mind, is trying to time her first metamorphosis for Walpurgis Nacht, next Tuesday that ever is."

"Oh, God," exclaimed Burgess in that horribly strangled voice so foreign to him, "oh. God, can nothing be done?"

I shook my head.

"At the moment nothing, old friend. Indeed we might defeat our own purpose by any premature action. We have got to prove our conclusions, however deeply we may ourselves believe and bank on our premises. Nevertheless, there is one strong gleam of hope in the situation for you, for all of us—if lycanthropy be acquired by extraneous means, such as I have detailed to you, such acquired lycanthropy can be equally exorcised with the will and consent of the impregnated person, and the impregnation can be purged. Keep that before your mind: and let us hope while there is hope. Now do you not agree with me, with Manders. that this hell-brood must be destroyed, wiped out. and put beyond the pale and possibility of further harm and deeds of ghastliness?

"Indeed I do," said Burgess fervently, with as much determination as ever a man put into his voice, "indeed I do. I am master of myself again. Line—you will be the first to understand and forgive this momentary weakness—and I will fight with every fibre of my being to save the soul and, I trust, the future life of Dorothy: for- as you have guessed. I love her."

I nodded and gripped his hand. as we stood on the terrace in the bright, baleful moonlight: and I heard, with a little shiver, the old blue clock over the entrance to the stable-yard strike midnight. It was the hour that we are ever most up against the unknown elementals, and the conditions were all favourable to them; but I intended to win against all the powers of evil arrayed against us, including the Prince of the Powers of Darkness himself, whatever the grim cost.

"Show me how to do it," he said simply, as the last of the twelve notes of the old clock died away.

"Come inside, and we'll go into the details of my plans," I answered, taking his aim and retracing our steps along the wide terrace, white in the silver light of the hard-hearted moon.

IV

We re-entered the library through the open window, which I closed behind me; and I marvelled at Burgess's wonderful recovery of control. Apparently he was as cool as though it were a normal evening and nothing untoward had been even mentioned. But his face was set, his lips compressed, and his indicative jaw pushed out—a fine firm. strong face, but one with which no one at the moment would have cared to play me fool or take liberties.

Manders and Blenkinsopp were in deep consultation, standing on the old Persian rug in font of the open wood fire.

A drink all round, I think," said Burgess, proceeding to play host, "and then to business. You fellows must excuse my absence, but the room was getting a bit hot for an open-air yokel like myself. Osgood here has been good enough to put me wise upon certain essential details; and I am now completely at your disposal without reservation. In fact. I am only too anxious, now that I am in with you, to pull rny full weight in the boat. I may add that I accept fully, and am convinced of the homble reality and truth of every word that has been spoken here in this room tonight. I cannot say more. Now, Line, what are your plans?" he asked, motioning us to our seats: and I was glad to see him light a cigar by instinct, as I knew that it would soothe his strained nerves.

We all resumed our chairs: and I set the ball rolling.

"My plans are largely subject to Blenkinsopp." I said. "but I trust that we shall see eye to eye." He made a gesture of assent. "I do not frankly anticipate active trouble of any sort before next Tuesday night— Walpurgis Nacht that is, coupled with full moon, an irresistible combination for such elementals and superphysicals—and my own view is that they are saving themselves up for a grand orgy on that notable occasion with, I frankly fear. the first metamorphosis of Miss Dorothy as part of their devilish programme, if she be sufficiently impregnated by then. At the new moon and at the first quarter the mutilation of sheep which has taken place, and is of itself characteristic of werewolf 'playfulness.' is all in keeping with my theory of heading up to a climax, which I anticipate with no small feeling of certainty at full moon, especially taking into consideration its conjunction with the great night of the year for all elemental and superphysical orgies—not least of all, human sacrifice. Therefore. I am laying my plans to meet and counter what will otherwise assuredly happen on that night. I anticipate a fresh raid that night from the Dower House, probably shortly before midnight: but, of course, we must be upon the spot earlier ourselves in case it should be earlier or the venture be planned farther afield than heretofore. Nothing must be left to chance."

"I propose." I went on. speaking calmly, but emphatically, "to shoot anything in animal form that emerges from the Dower House, and not only to shoot, but to shoot to kill—"I saw poor old Burgess start and clench his hand—"that is, in the case of two. If there be three werewolves, I shall plan, in the case of the third and smallest one, to shoot only to disable, preferably in the foot. I have all ready and waiting in this house half a dozen Winchester repeaters and the same number of Brownings; and I emphasize that at all hazards in the case of the two big wolves, which I anticipate with no small certainty, it must be death.

"As for the shooting-party, of course. Blenkinsopp, as official referee, must stand aside—"

" Unfortunately, damn it," he broke in most unofficially.

"But," I went on. "there will be Manders. Burgess, and myself."

"I will take the smallest wolf." struck in Burgess with a prompt determination, which I fully appreciated. "It must be left to me."

"It shall." I said emphatically, realizing his reason: "so don't worry any more on that score. I will take the biggest myself."

"Pere Garou," interpolated Manders, with his ever cynical little touch. "And old Anna, the gaunt she-wolf, who might have been foster-mother to Romulus and Remus, thus falls to my bow and arrow?"

"Of that I am not altogether sure," I interrupted. "We must have a shooting squad at the front- door, and an auxiliary one to cover a possible exit at the back, though I fancy myself that the sortie will take place from the front and through the gap in the hedge. That has not been repaired yet, has it?" I asked, turning to Burgess.

"No, not yet." he answered: "but I gave orders for it to be done this afternoon."

"Well, please have them countermanded first thing to-morrow morning for a day or two, old chap," I said. "I won't want to arouse the least suspicion or chance any of my plans going agley. No, my dear Manders. with your kind consent I propose to put you in charge of the back-door squad, as I must have someone there whom I can rely upon absolutely. You can be round with us in no time. once the shooting begins."

"Just as you wish," he acquiesced, with that prompt self-effacement and cordiality that helps generalship so much. "I'm entirely at your disposal in the matter, though for preference I would love a shot at old Pere Garou. He has got on my nerves and makes me itch to rid the earth of his foul presence every time I think of him—phew!"

"And your other guns?" asked Burgess quietly.

"I would have preferred them all amateur." I answered, "but I shall be one short. I propose to enlist Verjoyce and Wellingham to-morrow, and put them under Manders' command at the back. They are a couple of real sporting white youngsters, and both excellent shots, as I have taken the trouble to find out for the third gun at the front, I am a bit at a loss."

"Hedges," said Burgess promptly, "he, like Jevons. was bom and brought up on the estate, and both went through the Boer War with me in the Yeomanry: and I would trust them both absolutely and without reservation. I will guarantee both of them to do anything I do or tell them to do, and not to talk."

"Right," said I: "then Hedges let it be. That takes a weight off my mind,"

"I will talk to Verjoyce and Wellingham." volunteered Manders, "if you chaps like. I know them a bit better than you do now, and they have got a bit of a respect for my views and opinions." he added, with a laugh; "and I'll call in Blenkinsopp to give it a proper convincing official air. They will come in quick enough, you may be sure. if there is any excitement going."

"Splendid," I agreed: "and Burgess shall tackle Hedges, and I think that Jevons should be told as well, as we are pretty sure to want his help, if only to cover up our tracks. I will get out a plan and work out all details: and on Sunday evening we will have a consultation. Further, without wishing in any way to be melodramatic. I would suggest an oath of secrecy, which will at least impress the youngsters and the men of the great seriousness of the undertaking."

"Yes, I am quite with you there," said Blenkinsopp. "It is quite as well and can do no possible harm."

So it was agreed.

"And now to bed," I said. "We all need our rest, and we shall want our nerves in the best possible order on Tuesday night. Our plans are now well forward, thank God."

And thus we broke up; and before turning into bed I took one long last look at the cold face of the moon out of my window, wondering what she at her hour of fullness was destined to bring forth.

V

The next day, Saturday, the twenty-seventh, was beautifully bright and sunny, a glorious morning: and I spent the early part of it in the garden with Aim until she had to go in to read to Bullingdon. as I found she often did.

"The nurses tell me that he quite looks forward to it," she said naïvely, as we finished a grand review of the tulips, which were all coming up in fine formation against the impending arrival of May.

"I've no doubt, my dear." said I a trifle cynically. "I would stay in bed every morning myself, if only I could guarantee nice girls to come up and read to me; but I suppose that I'm not pale or interesting or good-looking enough to attract them."

"Line, you're a perfect beast," exclaimed Ann, blushing hotly: "and here have I been wasting half my valuable morning taking you round the garden and being polite to you."

"Nothing more than common decency demands, and your duty as hostess, my dear Ann; and you know that both Burgess and I have spared no effort in the past to instil nice manners into you from the days when you were a shocking little hoyden."

Ann made a face at me,

"There, that shows how unsuccessful you have been. Never again will I waste a single moment upon such an unappreciative and unattractive person. Mr. Osgood!"

And with a sarcastic curtsey she turned on her heel and ran down the terrace and in at the hall-door, singing a merry little snatch that belied her simulated disdain.

I followed more slowly, refilling my pipe. and entered by the library window.

There I found Manders and Burgess talking.

"Do you know." said the former, obviously interested, "that Clymping here has Just been taking the wind out of our cosmopolitan sails, after all. by telling me that what we had forgotten in our town surroundings and wider spheres is still extant amongst the country folk in their lore, and firmly believed in by them nowadays? Not exactly werewolves." he added, "but hell-hounds, which are at least first cousins and much the same thing for all practical purposes, in fact, you remember when Llewellyn slays poor old faithful Gelert. he cries 'Hell-hound, by thee my child devoured,' when the old dog has been actually killing the hell-hound or werewolf—'a great wolf all torn and dead— tremendous still in death.'"

"Yes." broke in Burgess, "for once I did not sleep much last night, a strange feeling for me, turning the whole thing over and over again in my mind and viewing it from every angle; and it came back to me irresistibly that. even in these days in England, the old rustic population in many places still believe in 'the hell-hounds.' and there are cases even recently of their hearing them, like a pack in full cry— perhaps not so much in Sussex- which is alas, fast becoming suburbanized by the spreading of London, its handiness to town, motorcars, and the whole trend of things—but in parts more remote and farther west, for instance. Modern board-school education, with its intensely prosaic outlook, has had a devastating effect upon folk-lore and rustic tradition; yet. despite it, the older yokels remember, even if they do not talk too openly to mere strangers about such things for fear of ridicule, secretive 'with two soul-sides, one to face the world with' and the other that harbours the traditions of their forefathers. Hell-hounds are to- day believed in in many secluded cottage homes, where a night outing is regarded as something of a spiritual adventure, a thing not to be lightly or unadvisedly undertaken. Only recently, in the Times itself, a correspondent quoted the case of a servant girl who turned back to her cottage home after her evenmg out, because she heard the hell-hounds and dared not face the malign spirits in desolate places ready to spring out upon incautious travellers."

"And I suppose her unimaginative mistress sacked her the next day?" commented the ever-cynical Manders. with his characteristic little laugh.

"That is very interesting indeed," I said, strangely gratified by this unexpected touch of confirmation so near home, "and quite a new viewpoint to me. Though tradition undoubtedly dies hard, it would seem to show that the werewolf has not so long been an unknown form of spiritual projection in this county as one thought, although unrecognized in its infrequent manifestations,"

For a short time we discussed the question: and then I turned to Burgess.

"Now then, old chap. what I came in to do was to sketch out a map of the Dower House and its surroundings, upon which to draw out in detail our plan of action. It will help to show everyone his exact post at the critical moment without any talking and moving about, which might be heard and arouse suspicion. At such times such super-physicals are apt to be acutely supersensitive. Can you give me a suitable large piece of paper?"

"An excellent scheme." Burgess cordially agreed. "Come into my own particular sanctum, and I'll fix you up all right: and there on the wall you will have the ordnance map of the whole estate, with the Dower House bit as big as you will want for your purposes."

So leaving Manders to stroll out on the terrace, we went across the hall to a pleasant panelled room in the right-hand comer facing the drive. It was the most comfortable room in an essentially comfortable house, full of odd easy chairs, with a couple of low deep couches, a big writing-table in the window, and another in the middle of the room, at which Burgess transacted all his estate business. One wall was partially covered by the big map he had referred to, flanked by two old Chippendale tallboys, holding papers, while a big cupboard in the corner, which was in reality a safe, held all sorts of deed-boxes and the unsightly paraphernalia of record and organization—the whole being concealed by panelling, which opened back on hinges. Round the other walls were prints, photographs, and sporting trophies, mostly of a more personal than actual value, and over the mantelpiece was a big cigar-cupboard—a regular man's room arranged for comfort and business, combined with an eye to privacy and especial confidences in a house full of guests.

It was there, if not in the hall, that Ann and he and I always sat in the evenings, when quite alone.

"That's just the thing," I said, exarmning the big map. "It will help to keep my proportions accurate."

Burgess soon had me fixed up and left me to my plan. Fortunately I have a bit of a knack for sketching and architectural work: and it did not take me long to rough out a small one, upon which I marked in the individual places roughly for discussion. And in a little over an hour I had the larger sketch ready as well. but without any places put in, leaving that until after a general conference upon the subject, to see what other suggestions might be offered.

I had just finished and rolled up my smaller drawing, lest perchance it might fall into the wrong hands and arouse any sort of suspicion—the larger one did not matter so much, as it was a plan pure and simple—when I heard the angry eructations of a Klaxon, as a car turned in at the gates: and soon a long, low "ninety" Mercédès, with a wonderful white body. bounded up the drive with Harry Verjoyce, recognizable only by impression in his overall touring-coat and goggles, at the wheel, and Bill Wellingham beside him. They were instinct with life and audacity, ever on the look-out for what they termed "fun," which might mean anything so long as it spelt a new sensation preferably spiced with danger; and I knew that there I had the right stuff, especially when, under the veneer of abandonment and carelessness, there was the discipline of the Guards to work upon.

I went out into the hall and found Burgess greeting them as they pulled off their driving-coats over their heads and revealed the very latest things in tweeds and silk socks underneath.

"What about the old Mere, Mr. Clymping?" asked Verjoyce, "I've left the engine running, as she's the devil to start. Shall I take her round to the garage, as she's got a bit of ginger under her bonnet and isn't so easy to tackle till you know her little ways?

"Right-oh," said Burgess, laughing like a schoolboy, which did him good. I could feel. "I'll come round with you myself and show you the way, as I'm always interested in big cars, while Osgood here can mix us one of his famous bronxes against our return."

Soon we were all assembled in the hall. outwardly a cheerful enough party as usual, but with the horror ever lurking in the background, of which so far the two youngsters and Ann were happily ignorant.

"One of you may see Lord Bullingdon when he has had his nap after lunch—that is, probably about three o'clock—" announced Ann officially: "but the doctors think it better that it should not he both the first time. You will have to settle it between yourselves."

"It'd better be Bill," said Harry Verjoyce promptly. "He's better at these things than I am."

"These things" was eminently vague; but we all had an instinct what he meant and what it covered.

"Right-oh." said young Wellingham gruffly; "here's luck."

And he swallowed his cocktail to cover his feelings: and Manders came to the rescue again with some questions about the big white Mercédès racer, which was Verjoyce's latest addition to his auto-stud and a very safe topic.

And then lunch, itself a merry enough meal. at which the ball was tossed about from one to another with the deliberate purpose of banishing unpleasant things to the background of memory; and I never met a better man at the game than Manders, who always seems to have the knack of the right note to keep things at the required pitch.

"I will call you, Mr. Wellingham," Ann said, leaving us over the port, "when you can see Lord Bullingdon; but don't stay more man ten minutes, please, and keep him off unpleasant subjects as much as ever you can. We want to keep the circumstances surrounding the shock as much out of his mind as we can."

Ann put on a professional manner which was quite becoming, and would have been amusing if the circumstances had not been so grave—I might say appalling.

"I'll do my best, Miss Clymping," said Bill Wellingham, holding the door open for her. "Trust me, though I'm afraid a poor wretched subaltern can't be counted on for the tact, to say nothing of the airs and graces, of these barrister chaps."

It was quite happy, and allowed Ann to leave us in the midst of a general laugh.

"All right, my lad," said Manders, laughing, "I'll get back to you before I've done. I often hope myself that there's more affectation than real idiocy amongst the junior officers of the Guards' Brigade."

Then Blenkinsopp spoke, introducing a more serious vein.

"Could you two chaps get two or three days leave for a very particular' purpose," he asked— "say from Monday to Wednesday or Thursday? It's rather important; and I'll explain the whole business later on."

"Might be wangled, Bill, mightn't it?" said Harry Verjoyce.

Wellingham nodded.

"Think so. We've both been very good boys lately, and doing quite a lot of beastly duty one way and another."

"Well then," said Blenkinsopp quietly, "I'll put you wise after Wellingham has seen Bullingdon. It's man's work I want of you both, no kid's game: and it's connected with the cleaning up of this infernal business.

The boys started; and their faces instantly grew serious, assuming a new and very businesslike look.

"Then it's got to be done," they said in chorus. "We're game, you can bet."

"It may be a shooting matter," added Blenkinsopp. "Can you chaps shoot?"

"Some." replied Wellingham succinctly, pursing his lips, "and as for old Harry, he's a topper, not only high birds, but big game in Africa with his guv' nor once, lucky devil, before the old man got laid out by a rhino."

I recalled the incident a year or two back.

And then we talked on neutral subjects, such as Wellingham's legitimate grievance against his Irish tenants, who refused to pay their rents and finance him as an officer in the Guards should be financed, and Verjoyce's views of the unfair incidence of taxation upon the "upper rich," till Ann looked in at the door.

"He's waiting for you. Mr, Wellingham." she said in her dear. soft voice. "Come along."

And Wellingham clicked to attention with that serious look on his face I had liked so much all along. I knew instinctively that there was the right stuff in the lad all through—in both of them, I may say—despite their deliberately cultivated carelessness of manner and frivolity of outlook upon such a boring subject as life.

VI

The rest of us adjourned to the library when Wellingham went upstairs, and strolled up and down the terrace until his return less than a quarter of an hour later, all worried and anxious and glad to get on the move.

His face was white, and I could see that it was a bit of an effort to keep it from twitching. "Poor old Tony-Boy" he said with more feeling than he wanted to show, as we all returned to the library, "he looks fearfully knocked out and as white as a ghost—more like a girl than a man; and it knocked me over a bit to see him like that. He was always so full of life and go, and the first over the top in every harum-scarum joy-ride."

[Memo. Here let me, as chronicler, interpolate that at Wellingham's special request, and not deeming it essential. I have agreed to reproduce, in a few words, what he told us, instead of asking him this time to make a separate document of it.]

"He couldn't give me a grip." he went on, "hardly a squeeze: and it seemed to comfort him to hold my hand like a girl. and all he said at first was 'dear old Bill' twice, in such a small soft voice that a great lump came into my throat, and I'm damned if I didn't want to blub like a new kid at school. I couldn't speak, and just patted his white hand, which you could almost see through, like a sentimental lunatic, and then it was all I could do to keep from bursting out laughing at myself."

He took out a yellow silk handkerchief with crimson bull-dogs on it and wiped his lips, a bizarre contrast to his emotion.

"Give me a cigarette. Harry, old top," he said; and as he lit it, he seemed to get a fresh grip on himself. "It was too beastly for words, as the poor old chap wanted to get at what had happened. I told him there had been an accident, and he said he didn't remember anything about it: and then—oh, my God, then he asked after poor old Wuffles, and was most insistent. Not that he was in love with her really, you know, though at first he thought he was, and then she complicated matters by falling in love with him, which wouldn't surprise anyone in the least who knew old Tony, but he felt some sort of responsibility. And at last, when he would have it and forced my hand. I told him she had been killed—that was all. I didn't tell him anything more, except that it was painless. His face was contracted horribly for a moment, and then he squeezed my hand ever so weakly and said, 'Thank, you, Bill, old boy'—in such a weak pathetic little voice—leave me now; but come and see me again to-morrow, if you can. and Harry too."

"You shall," said Burgess warmly, "if you'll stay the night. We shall he delighted."

"It's top-hole of you," answered Wellingham, "if we may. We've got no glad-rags with us, though—not even a tooth-brush."

"Never mind that." said Burgess cheerfully. "We'll fix you up with pyjamas between us: and I always regard spare tooth-brushes in any house as much a necessity as spare parts in a good garage."

And so it was fixed: and I "wirelessed" across to Blenkinsopp to put off his explanation till the evening, as I could see that the boy was a bit overwrought.

VII

We heard voices on the terrace, those of Ann and Dorothy, to whom we introduced the two youngsters, while Ann assured us that Bullingdon was all right. He had appeared exhausted, but the nurse on duty—herself I found out afterwards—had given him a little brandy; and he had fallen asleep almost at once.

Dorothy struck me as appearing pale and overdone, with great black circles under her blue eyes, but looking more beautiful than ever, if possible, with her lips startlingly bright and vivid.

"You don't look very fit," I said in a low voice, which could only be heard by Burgess, whom I caught eyeing her anxiously.

"I have been sleeping so badly the last few nights and having such queer dreams," she answered in a low voice. "My father won't let me have the blinds down—it's his latest fad—— and the moon is so bright, streaming right across my bed. It makes me so restless; and I am quite growing to hate the moon. It seems to have such a strange influence over me."

Burgess and I shot a quick glance across at each other.

"My father is in one of his ecstatic moods—almost ferocious, and wandering about the house like a caged animal." the girl went on; "and at times I am quite afraid of him. I know it's very silly: but somehow I can't help it."

I could see mat Burgess was keeping a strong grip upon himself: and I laid a warning hand on his arm.

"And your old Anna?" I asked with assumed carelessness. "How does she take these things?

"Oh, she is much the same as usual, only a bit more surly and unapproachable, if possible," replied Dorothy, with a little shiver, which showed that her nerves were overwrought and out of order. "You see, she is thoroughly accustomed to my father's queer ways, as he is to hers. I felt as though I should scream or have hysterics or do something silly, if I didn't get away from it all; so I came up to have tea with Ann."

"Why, you're shivering, poor child," said Burgess with unusual emotion. "Come indoors: we'll have tea at once. I can't have you catching cold."

In the warmth of the hall amidst the more cheerful smroundmgs Dorothy soon began to recover tone and become her natural self again; and Burgess was most attentive protective way, which made her look up at him with big, pathetic, grateful eyes.

"It's so nice to be made a fuss of." she said, laughing for the first time—a little queerly, I thought, that laughter which is on the borderland of tears. "I shall go home much better and hap- pier; and then I shall be able to sleep to-night."

"Of course you will," I said soothingly: and then the conversation became general, with the usual chaff and laughter, until she became taken out of herself and grew quite natural again, youth responding to youth and the glow of cheerful surroundings.

"I wish you could stop on with us and help Ann with all these men?" ventured Burgess, when she got up to leave, as the old grandfather clock in the comer of the hall chimed a quarter to six. "I will go down and get your things, if you will give me a note to the Professor."

A look of eagerness came over her face: but it died out instantly, "I daren't—really." she answered gratefully, "much as I would love to. My father made me promise to be not later than six, and he will be angry as it is. If I suggested stopping the night he would make a very angry scene, and come up himself and take me home; and I would not like you to see him in one of his strange, fierce moods. He can't help them at times," she added loyally "I suppose it is the penalty of genius."

Burgess offered no comment, simply bowing to her decision.

"You shall not be late," he said encouragingly. "I am going to drive you down myself and will see to that."

"You are too good," she murmured in a low voice—for him alone.

VIII

That night, after Ann had gone to bed, again warned off early much to her disgust, though she realized that there was a serious reason behind it, as both Burgess and I had explained to her— and I must say she took it in a very sporting fashion—Blenkinsopp and Manders invited Wellingham and Verjoyce into the library, while Burgess and I adjourned to his own room to go over my plan before presenting it to the others.

"We can manage quite well without you." said Blenkinsopp considerately. "These lads won't be very hard to convince when they know that we all four firmly believe in what we say, and that it is even unofficially recognized at the Yard, especially as the hot-blooded sympathy of youth is already aroused; and you must be dead sick of repeating the facts again and again, my dear Osgood, while to Clymping it must be personally specially distasteful. You and he can be getting on with the practical side of the job. I'll give you a call. probably within an hour; and you can add anything that may appeal to you or appear necessary or advisable."

In his sanctum poor old Burgess showed more emotion than in all the years of our long friendship I had ever seen him exhibit.

"By God, Line, old man. think of that poor girl in that hell-house amidst such ghastly, unnatural surroundings. I felt to-night as though I could not leave her; but she wouldn't let me even come up me drive. Her father is so wild and queer, she says, poor child, without ever drearmng of the inner horror of the whole accursed thing. What was I to do?" he concluded, throwing out his hands dramatically in a way utterly foreign to him, which brought home to me how deeply the iron of circumstances had entered into his soul.

"Nothing, old friend, nothing," I said as gently as I could—"the hardest thing of all to do in times of stress; but we would assuredly spoil everything by anything premature. Remember, the ground under our feet is still very insecure from the outsider's point of view; and we must wait for proof positive before we dare act without fear of the reaction of ridicule and a horrible bungling of everything. We could never then hope to rescue Dorothy. This old Pere Garou, as Manders always calls him, would simply laugh in our faces and remove her without trace, transhipping to some spot off the map, sad leaving us high and dry, hoist on the petard of our own precipitancy."

I paused; and he nodded gloomily.

"Smoke, old man." I said. to break the tenseness of things, "and you might give me a drink before I go on to two other important things in my mind. You would be the better for one yourself. I noticed that you took practically nothing at dinner; and. if you go on like this, you won't sleep again to-night, just when your nerve armd your hand must be at then' steadiest—for Dorothy's sake."

He did as I suggested: and. when he had lit his cigar, I went on.

"It is no good beating about the bush. Burge. I am morally certain that those devils in human shape, evil spirits in human cases, have impregnated Dorothy"—I saw him clench his hands and bite his lip—"and, therefore, it is up to us all the more to save her. I frankly anticipate that under their foul tutelage, against her own knowledge and against her will, she will metamorphose for the first time on Tuesday. That is why I am glad that of your own accord you chose the small wolf as your mark; for thus it will be your own hand that will maim or lame to save or wound to cure. You can leave the rest to me. Her soul I will save as surely as those elemental fiends have plotted to damn it now and for all eternity. Poor Dorothy will, alas, have to pass through the fire in more senses than one; but she will, by God's good grace, in the end come out purified of all taint. You trust me?"

Burgess gripped my hand till I thought the blood would jump from beneath my nails; and I was truly thankful with he relaxed pressure.

"God bless you. Line. and help you, my friend in direst need."

"And now. Burge. there is yet one thing more I have to break to you—a thing which, outside the human side, will hit you as deeply as anything else. or would have done a day or two ago."

I paused. I could hardly get my own lips to phrase such ghastly vandalism: but we were dealing with things more ghastly and more vital than mere bricks and mortar.

"We shall have to burn the Dower House with all its contents to the ground—reduce it to a heap of ashes,"

Again Burgess started, but almost as promptly subsided, shrugging his shoulders. His most treasured possession on earth, his lifelong idol, cherished and nurtured by a great sense of atavism, had faded into the immaterial beside the greater things of the moment and the one supreme absorbing necessity of saving Dorothy, who was now the whole world to him. In comparison all things else had lost all sense of counting and had assumed negligible proportion.

"The only way of extirpating a werewolf absolutely, of getting finally quit of the spirit of the elemental after having slain the mere case." I went on, trying to talk as though it were an everyday affair, "is to burn the body itself and reduce it to ashes. Burial is a ghastly error. A single bone of itself may attract and retain the elemental; and the superphysical will live on for centuries. Further, the only way to be assured that no kindred elemental spirits survive in the old surroundings and haunt them unseen, is to burn to the ground any dwelling once inhabited by them. So we shall thus kill two birds with one stone, so to speak: and. not only that, to the world it will merely be made known that the wonderful old Clymping Dower House, a gem of Tudor architecture built upon the site of the old castle, was on the night of Tuesday, April 30. burnt to the ground, and in it perished the famous German professor. Herr Lycurgus Wolff. and his old servant, Anna Brunnolf. His daughter, Dorothy, was luckily got out of the house, and rescued just in time by the house-party at the Manor, who happened to be out on the terrace just before turning in to bed and were attracted to the spot by the flames—including Major Blenkinsopp of Scotland Yard, who will give the story his cachet. You grasp the importance of this?"

Burgess had his head buried in his hands, but looked up as I concluded.

"What must be, must be," he said with Æschylean simplicity, grasping the sense of inevitability that is the keynote of real tragedy. "If it will save Dorothy and her soul, it is dirt cheap at me price."

I nodded. The man was great in the greatness of his simplicity and his love—never a thought of himself, and accepting the great price without whine or whimper or even a cavil: and I, of all people, knew how much it meant to him.

Then I showed him my plan of the position of the guns, detailed suggestions for arranging with Hedges for a supply of dry wood to be on the spot, together with plenty of petrol, and suggested that his chauffeur, Wilson, should be sent up to town on Tuesday to buy new tyres, or anything else that might be wanted, and be given the night off. Hedges and Jevons he must see personally and trust with the whole story the next afternoon, while Manders and Blenkinsopp took the two youngsters for a walk through the woods, and. as though casually, showed them the Dower House and its surroundings, possibly passing the time of day with Dorothy and even the Professor, if necessary.

Burgess agreed, and approved my plan of the guns, thoroughly himself again now that we were on the fringe of action; and we were all ready when Manders tapped lightly at the door and called us through to the library

"The lads are splendid," he said with real appreciation— "never jibbed once, and took it like an assault-party receiving their orders. They made some quaint comments, the dear boys, but it never occurred to them to doubt a single word spoken by a man like Blenkinsopp. By gad, they're as game as young fighting-cocks."

We rose and followed him into the library with the plans in our hands,

"Major Blenkinsopp has told you everything connected with this ghastly business?" I said, noting there two faces, strangely serious for once. "Is there anything I can add?"

"Nothing at all, thank you," answered Wellingham, as usual acting as spokesman for the pair. "He has made it all too horribly plain and convincing: and you can count on both of us—to death, if need be, though I hate talking that kind of cheap melodramatic tosh, you know. It's up to us not only to help to save Miss Wolff, but to avenge poor old Wuffles and old Tony's narrow escape. These"—he paused for a word—"these filthy unclean things must be wiped out once and for all time."

Harry Verjoyce nodded.

Old Bill's right, as usual," he said solemnly and then he lit a cigarette, as though be had forgotten something important.

"We knew we could count upon you two chaps," I said appreciatively, and men without farther to-do I produced my plans and explained the positions, and told them moreover about the climax of the holocaust, necessary not only to cover our tracks and account for the disappearance of Professor Wolff and Anna Brunnolf, but to eradicate all taint finally and for ever. Blenkinsopp agreed.

"Having got me to countenance shooting in my official capacity, you now ask me to assent to the second greatest crime in our modern decalogue at the Yard." he said— "arson. I mean: but I must admit that it seems to be most apt and necessary in this case, if Clymping will make the sacrifice—"

"With all my heart." broke in Burgess without reservation—a man of one fixed purpose.

"And," went on Blenkinsopp. "it will certainly do away with much subsequent awkwardness and things difficult to account for satisfactorily. The fire of itself will occasion publicity enough, both on account of the Professor's name in scientific circles and on account of its proximity to the Brighton Road mysteries, but my presence and that of Inspector Boodle will avert any suspicion. But it seems a woeful thing to have to do." he added regretfully. "A small thing in comparison." said Burgess with cold decision. Since Dorothy had been brought into the matter so directly and acutely nothing else seemed to matter in his eyes.

And so we sat round me table, completing our plans and working out positions till bedtime.

"I will take the front of the house. Osgood." said Blenkinsopp. "with Clymping. yourself, and the keeper, and put Boodle at the back with Manders. Wellingham. and Verjoyce. I fancy, with you, that the exit is more likely to be from the front than the back, but. of course, we can't be sure. I will arrange for two more C.I.D. men I can trust absolutely to be on the spot, one at the entrance to the drive, and the other handy with the man with the wood and the petrol. Mutton I shall get rid of by sending him some miles down the road to divert the traffic, giving him specious enough reasons of my own, and the local inspector I'll put on a similar job somewhere up the road. That will not only get them out of harm's way, but will make them feel highly important, while it will prevent them spotting the fire and coming to the rescue prematurely before it has time to get such a hold that no one will ever be able to put it out."

"Excellent." I agreed cordially. "It doesn't seem to leave a loophole for trouble or the premature good offices of the well-intentioned police; and we can't afford one in this instance.

And so, satisfied that things were as far ahead as possible, and shaping themselves as well as could be for the climax of the hideous drama, we all went to bed with the sense of a good day's work accomplished.

That night, as had become my habit during me last fortnight, I pulled up my blind and watched the cold face of the moon all but come to maturity, and thought, with a heavy heart full of sympathy, of the poor lonely girl lying full in its baleful light in her bed in that horrible house, once so dear to me and now so loathsome; and I knew that Burgess's thoughts were there, too.

IX

The next day, Sunday, was again perfect; and in the glorious spring sunshine it did not seem possible that there could be such evil so close at hand on the very doorstep, so to speak, only going to prove our daily proximity to the door of the apparently unreal, which is, perhaps, often very real, if beyond our immediate understanding and intelligence. We all spent it in a delightful desultory fashion, talking of everything except the subject uppermost in our minds, and making up to Ann for the neglect of the previous two evenings. That is, all except Blenkinsopp, who thought it high time to take Boodle into his full confidence and explain everything to him in detail; and they were closeted together most of the rnorning, preparing a private report for Sir Thomas Brayton and putting everything down in black and white.

At noon Wellingham was again allowed to see Tony Bullmgdon for a short time, and reported him much better and more cheerful. He seemed easier in his mind and worrying less, and he did not once refer to Miss Yvette St. Clair. His only reference to the accident was obviously dictated by the physical and mental lethargy of extreme weakness.

"Can't remember anything about any accident. Bill, old boy," he said almost pathetically. "One day—when I'm better—you must tell me all about it—and..."

And then he faltered and stopped, his mental energy
petering out. "I told him not to try," said Wellingham. who
all along had struck me as a very sound, sensible chap
under his happy-go-lucky, dare-devil exterior, "and talked
to him about odds and ends that didn't matter a tuppenny
cuss: and he seemed quite sorry when Nurse Clymping—
wifh a cheeky grin at Ann, which restored the balance of
things— "ordered me off the course."

"You shan't be allowed in again, if you are impudent. Mr.
Wellingham," said Ann severely, trying to look very
dignified. "Anyhow. it's Sir Harry's turn at half-past two—
that is, if you haven't already over-tired Lord Bullingdon
too much with your silly talk or thrown him back again,"
she concluded viciously.

"Right-oh, Miss Clymping." he laughed. "Harry's the lad
with the bedside manner—sort of Sir Humphrey Bedell at
6st.71b."

After lunch Verjoyce saw the invalid for a few minutes,
and announced that he had "bucked him up no end": and
Bullingdon certainly seemed easier and better for having
seen his two old "pals" and having broken the ice about
Miss St. Clair's death.

When he came downstairs, Blenkinsopp, Manders. and
the two youngsters went out, according to programme, and
brought off a very successful raid upon the Dower House,
meeting Dorothy by luck in the woods, and boldly asking
her permission to walk through the grounds and look at the
house, of which they had heard so much.

"We won't go in or think you rude if you don't ask us,"
said Manders, making it easier for her; "so we shan't
interrupt the Professor's working fever or make ourselves in
any way a nuisance. Architecture is quite a hobby of mine."

And for nearly half an hour they dawdled round both the
back and the front of the old Tudor house, ostensibly
listening to a lecture upon stone mullions and the phases of

the Tudor period from Manders. whilst in reality they were studying the ground, and each one marking down accurately his position. And Blenkinsopp reported afterwards that he had never reconnoitred more successfully under the unsuspecting nose of the enemy, though the dour face of old Anna followed them round with morbid suspicion, first appearing at one window and then at another— grim and ghoulish.

"All's fair in love and war," said Manders in a little aside to me; "and, if I be not in error, this is a case of both."

I nodded.

"It is indeed," I said with the fervour of conviction—"to the very death."

Burgess had meanwhile been closeted in his own room with Hedges and Jevons, while Ann had taken me out for a walk round the other side of the estate—manœuvred by myself for the good of my digestion, as she said. alleging that I had been eating too much and taking no exercise. Perhaps she was right. I had not had much time; and I am not a crank or a lover of what people call exercise simply for the sake of exercise. It is too much like an out-of-doors imposition, to my mental point of view. To some folk it has become a positive fetish or a form of self-immolation in this age of extremes from vice to virtue.

And so the hours sped on with the surface smooth and sparkling, the spring sunshine lending atmosphere and brightness, underneath which lay unutterable things ready and waiting to boil over at that psychological moment—to use Ann's much-derided phrase—which I hoped, with no small assurance, we had marked down to a nicety by the signs and portents at the disposal of our intelligence.

X

That night at ten o'clock, after a cheerful enough gathering for tea in the hall, with "snooker" afterwards till dressing-time, and then a most excellent dinner, we got to grips again with the impending horror in the library, dropping our everyday mask, so necessary before Ann and the rest of the household.

This time the party was bigger, with Boodle, Hedges, and Jevons added, standing to attention near the door with crude solemnity.

"Please sit down," said Burgess, pointing to chairs already set for them, "and remember that here to-night we are face to face with elemental facts, and each of us is a man and an individual. Circumstances make us all alike and equal; and the truest democracy of all is the realization of mutual respect and confidence. If anyone wishes to withdraw, now is the moment. We can all trust his silence and his honour: and I would be the last to wish to drag anyone into this ghastly business for my own or anybody else's sake."

Nobody spoke: and the men took their seats.

Then, after a slight pause. Jevons jerked out the obvious truth as though be could not help it "You know, sir, Hedges and I would follow you to hell."

It was crude and primitive, but struck the right note.

It's practically what it amounts to, old friend." said Burgess, with a grateful glance down the table at his two friends, though servants by circumstance.

To Boodle, who maintained a respectful official silence, it was all in the day's business.

And then we took the oath of secrecy—a mere formality, I felt. in such a loyal company of white men; and we laid our hands, one and all. upon the great Clymping farmly Bible, a great tome of priceless value—for in it, apart from its intrinsic value as a masterpiece of early printing, are there not written the names and the generations of the

House of Clymping. as they say in Holy Writ of other
genealogical trees?—and we swore as man to man before
God as our witness, that never would we for our own
purposes, or unless compelled by our duty as honest men
and citizens of Great Britain and its first cousin. America,
reveal any part of these happenings in which we were or
were to he personally and directly concerned—past.
present, and future,

And then Burgess, a great man that night and in
command, captain of his own soul and, maybe, of others,
rising to the occasion, lifted the great book off the centre of
the table and, replacing it in its case upon its own special
masterpiece of Chippendale sacred to it, said in a
wonderfully inspiring voice:

"Never has the House of Clymping been so honoured as
to-night by the great loyalty of Godfearing men."

And every heart in the room responded, feeling that he
had set the seal upon the oath.

And then we worked out with care and scrupulosity the
plans I had drawn up in conjunction with Blenkinsopp,
until each man knew precisely what was expected of him
individually, his moves in the forthcoming gambit of life
and death, not merely of bodies, but of human souls, and
his part in the inexorable battle against elemental evil.

And I marvelled at the great intelligence and constancy of
affection both of Jevons and of Hedges—old campaigners
with their master as well as boy comrades—to say nothing
of the quick grip of Boodle, the trained man; and I could
not help wondering why England—Britain, if you prefer
it—did not move quickly, more generally, and more
generously to recognize the material to hand in modern
democracy, as we do across the Atlantic.

Some day circumstances will arise in the cycle of history:
and she will—to her own eternal advantage.

XI

And then onwards things seemed to march rapidly, now all arrangements had been finally made and mutually agreed.

The next morning, as soon as it was light, Wellingham and Verjoyce left, as they were due on duty at nine o'clock and had to square the leave business at the same time; and I heard Blenkinsopp tell them, if there were any trouble, to "phone him. and he would see what he could do, as he knew their c.o. well. As a matter of fact. he fixed up in the end to go up with them in order to see his own Chief, arrange for the special men he wanted, and put the final touches upon things at headquarters: and never was Harry Verjoyce prouder than when he brought them safely back in time for tea. having "blinded" through every trap on the road. and having been rescued from the clutches of the police no less than three times by Blenkinsopp's badge.

Burgess and I had passed the morning, in conjunction with Hedges, with a little rifle practice, which Ann seemed to regard as a queer fad, worthy of our usual idiosyncracies—when I might have preferred the honour of driving into Crawley with her and hindering with the shopping.

That night it was early to bed for everybody and I felt grave and oppressed as I glanced out at the moon with her circle all but perfect. What would the next twenty-lour hours bring forth— for good or for evil?

And again I thought of poor tortured Dorothy, pale and restless, on the unconscious eve of things too hideous to contemplate.

XII

I can hardly bring myself in cold blood to write of Tuesday, April 30, a day burnt deep into my memory, which I would give much to forget.

All the morning we were all as flat as corked champagne after the first excess of gas, feeling the reaction of preparation, and loathing the compulsory inaction prior to the climax, upon which so much depended.

I made the opportunity of a talk with both Jevons and Hedges, while Wellingham and Verjoyce spent a little while with Tony Bullingdon. and gave him the latest gossip from the regiment. Blenkinsopp had a busy morning interviewing Mutton and many other policemen, including his two C.I.D. specials, and putting the last touches upon his official plans. Manders, with his usual inspiration, forced Burgess out of sheer politeness to take him over the estate. Ann, dear little Ann. played about happily at nurse, and did her best to bully the two usually irrepressible but decidedly depressed young subalterns backwards and forwards all over the place; and then she had the bad grace to vote them dull.

The afternoon began with rifle practice, apparently casually suggested to while away the time; and I could find no fault with the shooting of either Wellingham or Verjoyce, especially the latter, who could not go wrong.

Then, sending the lads in to tea in charge of Manders, we adjourned to the garage to superintend, in the arranged absence of Wilson. the packing of the luggage-van with petrol, the wood already having been arranged for by the ever-reliable Hedges.

This we left in charge of Boodle and the C.I.D. men, the fonner to join us on the spot at ten o'clock sharp.

Everything ready, we returned to the house; and Ann grumbled good-naturedly at our unsociability.

"I don't think I shall come down to dinner tonight," she said, with one of her quaint little faces—this had already been arranged by Burgess—"as I have a bit of a headache, and the company is not very tonic or inspiring."

"Poor old girl." said Burgess with more readiness of wit than usual, "don't bother about us. I tell you what. boys, if Ann doesn't feel up to coming down to dinner to-night, we'll take a night off and not bother to change. What do you say?"

It amused me, this bit of by-play for the benefit of the servants, as it was so contrary to every liking or instinct of Burgess's conventions and habits in the ordinary way.

"Rather." said I, chipping in. "I'm an uncivilized Yank who prefers tweeds and plenty to your dishes of herbs where glad-rags obtain. Let's have dinner early for once as well, may we?"

And so it was all settled; but, as Ann, headache-less and happy in her ignorance of things, kissed me good-night, she whispered:

"I'm jolly hungry all the same. Line, you beast. Think of poor dear little Ann sent off to bed by bad Brother Burge— with half a dozen quite nice men in the house, too! Is it to protect her, poor innocent little thing." I'm sure you all have some game up."

I only thanked God she had no conception what sort of game it was!

"You're a darling. Ann," I answered sympathetically. "I'll see that there are plenty of nice things sent up to you."

XIII

By half-past eight we were all gathered in the library. Dinner had been a strain on account of the presence of the servants; and we were all glad when it was over. We were all smoking hard at large cigars, which soothed us, as no smoking was the order once we starred.

I don't think anyone of us was nervous in the accepted sense of the word. but our nerves were as taut as elastic stretched parlous near breaking-point; but I think I may say that we were all fit and ready. We were all in rough tweeds and heavy overcoats, as it was quite cold, although the day had been warm enough, and we counted upon the prospect of a considerable wait; and, in addition to our repeaters, we each carried a Browning, a flask and a powerful electric torch— with the exception of Blenkinsopp and Boodle, who, in their official capacity, would not take rifles.

It had been arranged that either the former at the front or the latter at the back was to give the signal to fire, according to the door from which the exit was made——if any. That was almost the most anxious part of the whole business. I did not for an instant believe that my theory, now accepted without reservation by the others, could be wrong; but. if the line of action should fall out otherwise, it might land us in greater complications and deeper difficulties than ever.

Jevons was left in charge of the house with orders to close up and see everything quiet, to lock the library door after our departure, and to be generally prepared for anything or everything— and, if necessary, to keep up the illusion that we were all in consultation behind the locked library-door. At all costs he was to avert suspicion; and Burgess and I knew that we could trust his discretion.

"All ready?" asked Blenkinsopp quietly, as the hall-clock chimed a quarter to nine.

We all answered in the affirmative.

"Everyone understand his part?" he went on; "or has anyone any questions to ask? No more talking after this."

We all nodded. There were no questions.

All right." he said. "Now we will start."

And I will not deny that a keen thrill of anticipation went through me as we silently made our way through the long library window in single file.

Manders, Wellingham, and Verjoyce, under the guidance of Hedges, were to make their way through the woods to the back entrance, and to take cover amongst the trees just inside the garden near the little slip gate. Then Hedges was to work his way round the outside of the garden and join ns in the front.

Blenkinsopp, Burgess, and I were to take a wider sweep through the woods and come out in front, where Burgess and Hedges were to take cover under the wall by the gap, facing the front-door at an angle, with the moon full on the intervening ground. Blenkinsopp and I were to take up our position under the shadow of the last trees of the drive, immediately facing the old iron-studded oak door of the Dower House.

I shall never forget that long silent walk through the oppressive blackness of the woods, but it was infinitely less trying than the longer and even more silent, motionless wait after we had once all taken up our allotted positions; and it was a great relief, before ten o'clock, to see Hedges crawl through the gap and disappear under the shadow of the wall. where we knew Burgess to be awaiting him.

I do not think I ever remember a clearer or more lovely night outwardly, than this foul Walpurgis Nacht, with all the elemental and superphysical forces of evil out to revel in their great annual orgy of release. The moon was now full, and gave a wonderful white light; and the atmosphere was as clear as crystal.

It was indeed hard to believe that there was evil in the world—and, above all, such evil.

And so the time dragged on, each minute an hour, so it seemed, and the hours aeons. I could hear Blenkinsopp breathing deeply by my side during these interminable minutes that grew into first one hour and then another; and I expect that I was doing the same myself.

It was a relief when I felt his hand on my arm, and he showed me the dial of his luminous watch, indicating half-past eleven; and I nodded. And then my thoughts again turned to the youngsters on the far side of the grim old house, almost forbidding in the cold light, as though it had assumed a sinister aspect with its unconscious infection and I wondered how they were lasting out through the strain of the silent ordeal. Then my thoughts reverted to the house itself, its history amid its architectural beauty; and it seemed a strange, unnatural, almost horrible thought to think that within an hour or two—in all probability— it would be razed to the ground and reduced to a heap of ashes.

And then. as my thoughts wandered momentarily from point to point—it was just a quarter to twelve, Blenkinsopp told me afterwards—I felt his grip tighten upon my arm, and his breathing quicken.

I heard it. too. It was the sound of the clanking chain behind the old oak door with its great studs of iron. which divided the atmosphere of everyday life outside from the elemental drama of evil and unreality within. "Ah." breathed Blenkinsopp deeply, between his clenched teeth; and I gripped my repeater, my eyes glued fast upon the door.

XIV

Then came the longest wait of the last—seven minutes only, it was by the watch, as long as seven centuries none the less—and then came another sound from the direction of the old door; and then, in the clear brightness of the moon, it was pulled slightly ajar, leaving a dark gap to the left, a sinister black fissure in the front of the old house in the full white light.

And then... yes, I had been right in my bizarre theory, no fantasy, after all, of an ill-balanced mind... out of this black fissure issued a great grey male wolf with the low swinging stride of his species, clearly visible in the brightness of the moonlight.

I dropped on one knee and covered the ill-omened brute with my rifle.

And then ... I felt a constriction m my throat, and the veins on my temples knotted, as instinctively I wondered how poor old Burgess must be feeling . . . after the great grey male followed a smaller grey female wolf; and I knew that our worst fears were realities, and that the last crowning touch of hell's spite had been put to this piece of devil's work.

Dorothy had metamorphosed.

And in the awoke a burning desire, an intense passion to slay these foul things that had compassed it deliberately and wrought this desecration of her beautiful young body and the damnation of her pure white soul; and it nerved me as nothing else could ever have done.

And then appeared in the wake of the other two a gaunt brown old she-wolf, most sinister of all in the moonlight, and the two older ones formed up, one on either side of the younger one, as though to guide her unaccustomed feet along the dread path of damnation; and with long low sweeping strides they swung across the garden in formation towards the gap in the hedge, the grey male, to my delight, on the offside nearest to me, half a length in front.

Then he half-halted as though scenting danger, turning his head first to the right, and then to the left; and. as he stood still the incandescent bath of glowing moonlight, momentarily uncertain, and as splendid a target as though it had been daylight, Blenkinsopp's whistle blew—a long, shrill blast, sounding clear through the still night.

I drew a head on the old grey male and fired, and he dropped where he stood; and I thanked God as never before that my right hand had not lost its cunning.

Practically simultaneously two other shots rang out from beneath the shadow of the wall, and the old brown she-wolf dropped in her tracks, while the little one turned round with an almost human cry, yet half a yelp, and began to run back to the house, obviously terror-stricken, and limping in the near hind foot. And, as she reached the door-step, she gave another even more human cry, stumbled, and dropped.

We all rushed forward from our cover and ran across the garden, Burgess making straight for the old iron-studded door.

Can I describe what met my horror-stricken eyes, one of the most ghastly and gruesome sights God has ever allowed mortal vision to gaze upon. and one that time will never blot out? There lay the gaunt old she-wolf stark in death, a wolf and nothing but a wolf, with no sign of metamorphosing to her equally repulsive human shape; but the other nearer to me was a terrible and monstrous object, a man's body naked but hairy, with the head of a wolf and the feet of a wolf, not yet dead, but writhing as though in a ghastly convulsion.

As I approached he snarled viciously at me, baring his fangs and snapping furiously, wifh blood and froth on his horrid jaws; and he only just missed me. I drew my Browning and fired right at the heart of the foul hybrid creature without a touch of remorse, but rather with a great glow of triumph as I drew the trigger.

And then he gave yet one more convulsive wriggle and struggle: and I found myself standing over and staring down upon the dead body of Professor Lycurgus Wolff, which had housed so long to the detriment of the world and the cost of humanity the dread elemental that had projected itself that night.

"Thank God." I exclaimed fervently: and God knows I never felt more like praying in my life.

And then, as I heard steps racing round the house——it had all been the work of seconds, this climax of hours and weeks—I rushed forward to join Burgess on the steps of the house. I found him bending over the inanimate form of Dorothy, which he had wrapped round with his big coat with tender, concealing hands: and I felt for him in the great horror and great sacredness of the hour of his supreme ordeal,

"Thank God. she was her own true self when I reached her," he said in a strangled voice, "though unconscious. The wound is a mere trifle in the left foot; and I fancy she fainted from the shock. Keep the others back while I attend to it."

And, calling out to the rest to stand back. I gave him a light by my electric torch, while he washed the wound with antiseptic he had ready in his pocket, and bound it up with bandages from his first-aid case, which he had not forgotten; and I marvelled at the great thoughtfulness and tenderness of this big man in this prodigious test of mortal love. By the light of the torch, as I stood beside him. I noticed the unmistakable footprints of wolves' feet on the old stone step; but I hoped that Burgess in his absorption had overlooked them.

"We must get her away at once up to the house," he said in his firm, concentrated way. "She must remember as little as possible of this awful night, poor child. I won't give her any brandy till I get her right away."

"The C.I.D. men will be here in a moment with the van of petrol and the two-seater," I said. "One of the youngsters will drive you up and back again, if you care to return; and you can put her in Ann's charge—tell her it was the fire, or anything, but not to talk or ask questions. I don't think the wound will need a doctor. At any rate. I sincerely trust not."

The van and the car were on the spot almost immediately; and Wellingham drove off with Burgess beside him with his precious burden in his arms, wrapped round in his coat and mine, with an extra rug which I placed tenderly round her feet.

Then we turned to the grim work which lay in front of us—to make a pyre for the two horrible objects, grim and stark in the garden, and a holocaust of the once dear. but now tainted old house, together with all the elementals and superphysicals. such as would otherwise make it foul as their abiding-place for all time.

XV

In the car, Burgess told me afterwards in one of his rare moments of expansiveness, the girl had partially come to, but had easily been soothed, snuggling down happily into his arms, as though it had been the most natural thing in the world; and never again was there any doubt or question of how things stood between them.

And it was with a more or less happy heart, after all, that he handed over her sacred body into the tender keep of our splendid little Ann. who understood intuitively, and asked no questions out of love and loyalty to her idolized big brother.

"All explanations afterwards," was all he had said—this Ann told me. "Ask none and give none; but look after my darling for me."

And he was soon on his way back to join us, young Bill Wellingham driving like a man possessed in his desire to miss nothing.

XVI

Blenkinsopp had issued his orders; and, as soon as the
front door was clear, we all got to work piling up the dry
wood in the downstairs rooms and saturating it with petrol.
We also soaked the old woodwork of the building. sluicing
with petrol the glorious old beams, four centuries old. the
priceless panelling, and the carved staircase that was worth
its weight in gold, together with the miniature minstrels'
gallery, which was such a feature of the house, sung of by
architects as often as it had been sung in by musicians. The
beds, the curtains, the carpets were saturated with spirit
until the smell became almost overwhelming.

The two bodies—one outwardly an old man with a world-
wide reputation, the other apparently a she-wolf—were laid
upon special prepared pyres half way up the staircase, and
themselves saturated thoroughly in case anything should go
wrong with our plans: so that it might seem that, while
Dorothy escaped by her window and injured her foot in so
doing, the Professor and Anna had essayed the staircase
and been overcome by the consuming flames.

Last. but not least, we raised an immense pyre in the old
barn at the side, already half-full, as it stood, of
inflammable matter: and there we found not only human
bones, which we placed on top of the great heap, but a
woman's watch, which was afterwards privately identified
as the property of Mrs. Bolsover, and a diamond brooch,
which was recognized by Wellingham and Verjoyce as a
present from Tony to Miss St. Clair, and was actually
engraved on the back with the name "Wuffles."

These connecting and convincing proofs have never, I
may add. been made public by Scotland Yard, but lie hid in
its secret archives not in the superficial Black Museum, a
more or less polite pander to the morbid-minded public.

Burgess arrived back just before our preparations were concluded; and it was his own hand that set fire deliberately to the waiting pile, in order that no one else could ever be blamed. It was a wonderful sacrificial act, worthy of an enthusiast, but executed with the coolness and precision of a cricketer, without the least theatrical touch.

In the meantime I had had the whole horrid bed of lycanthropic flowers rooted up and placed upon the pyre in the barn: and I noted to instruct Hedges to see the whole hollow dug over deep, and buried in with quicklime, together with the noxious pools.

We opened the old mullioned windows to create a draught; and each of us did our share of the arson business from one point and another—the hall itself being voluntarily selected by Burgess, while I took the barn as my portion.

And in less time than it takes to write it there was one terrific concentrated blaze, which, within a few minutes, began to light up the skies despite the darkness and dankness of the low-lying hollow, fighting for supremacy with the ill-omened Walpurgis moon itself.

And with that caprice of thought that persistently obtrudes at really serious crises, we kept ringing through my head the whole time the historic words of Bishop Latimer to Bishop Ridley—"This day. brother, have we lit such a fire as shall never be put out."

But we dared not tarry long lest we should be caught upon the spot: so, collecting everything that might betray us. we packed the men aboard the van with instructions to return to the garage, while we took cover in the woods until such time as we dared reappear upon the scene and face our story out.

I need not labour detail or dilate upon the rest of that awful night, or rather early morning. Suffice to say, with Blenkinsopp and Boodle on the spot, our story, as we had anticipated, was never questioned. The local police dared not, even if it had occurred to them to do so: and to the reporters in due course, there was nothing to question with such a splendid three-colunm story to hand— literally red-hot—and the presses eager to lap it up.

Blenkinsopp drove straight back to town soon after six in the morning, when we had seen the house and barn burnt beyond all telling, the hollow a seething cauldron of furious ashes—angry perhaps, from the elemental fury within. He left Boodle in charge: and I need hardly add that he made things all right up at the Yard.

XVII

The sensation and the strain of the next few days were awful, and the reaction upon all of us great; but the worst was over, we all felt. whatever might befall.

Dorothy, with the vigour and recuperative power of youth, made wonderful progress, and her wounded foot was soon on the road to convalescence under the care of "Doctor" Burgess and "Nurse" Ann; and thereby we were saved taking an extra person, in the shape of a doctor, into our confidence upon this unpleasant and peculiarly secret subject.

Dorothy herself remembered nothing so far as the actual metamorphosis was concerned, and I doubt little that all along she had been under the hypnotic influence of the old Professor; but she had a mighty strange story to tell of the earlier happenings of the evening.

"We had no meals at all that day. and I was horribly hungry; but Anna said it was his orders, and would vouchsafe no further explanation. Then. as it grew dark and night approached, my father—and- oh. thank God, he was not my real father, only my stepfather, though he had forbidden me to say so to anyone, and I dared not do so before..."

A sudden light broke over my mind. It explained so much. Why had it never occurred to me, I wondered, as it made much that had been so puzzling quite clear.

"My real father was Colonel Cargill, of the Rifle Brigade," she went on: "but he died when I was a baby. and my mother before I was ten. Four years before her death she married Professor Wolff—why I could never make out. I have often thought during the last year that he must have hypnotized her. She was dreadfully unhappy; and I am sure that she was glad to die. if it had not been for me. Then for years I went from one school to another on the Continent and in this country, seeing practically nothing of him or that horrible old Anna Brunnolf "—the poor girl shuddered instinctively— "till they came to this country, when the Professor took me to live with them, refusing to allow me to communicate with any of my school friends or mistresses, and ordering me to call myself 'Dorothea Wolff' and him 'father,' and never on any account to disclose to anyone our real relationship. And I felt compelled against my will to obey him, as I was afraid of him." she concluded with pathetic simplicity,

Burgess's face lightened. There was one load off his mind in the fact that none of the old Professor's tainted blood ran in her veins, and the lycanthropic taint was thus beyond all doubt or question acquired and, therefore, exorcisable.

"Thank God," he said, taking her beautiful hand between his: and she smiled up happily into his eyes from her couch.

"He always had an extraordinary influence over me," she continued, "as over my mother—a ghastly, evil. penetrating influence that seemed to fascinate like a serpent's, and turned one's very soul sick. His eyes were so terrible at times; he had only to look at me, and I dared not cross his slightest wish. You remember that I told you how strange

he had been for a fortnight—from the new moon onwards?
That was forced from me by your sympathy; and I was in
mortal fear after I had spoken. Well. to cut things short, on
the evening of the fire, when it became dark all save for the
moon. he made me dip my hands and face in special water
that he brought with his own hands—strange water that
seemed to have a life of its own and was instinctively
repulsive. Then he placed round my waist a girdle of dark
plaited hair with a queer old gold buckle, and put flowers—
those horrible yellow ones with the black pustules, of
which Mr. Osgood destroyed one in the garden that
afternoon, and red and white ones as well; and then in the
old oak hall. empty and lit only by the light of the moon
through the mullioned windows, with white chalk he drew
a circle some six or seven feet in diameter, and placed me
in the centre, sprinkling my forehead, rny hands, and my
breast with some of the same water.

"Then"—and her face grew frightened at the horror of the
recollection, and I saw Burgess's grip upon her hand
tighten reassuringly—"he began in his rough guttural voice
to chant a weird incantation, moving slowly round and
round me all the while.

"I felt that he was mad- or worse: but I was fascinated
and could not move. Then he went across to the wood fire
burning on the open hearth, under the Clymping coat of
arms and took off an iron-pot, swinging it like a censer, and
sprinkling the whole centre of the circle, including myself,
with it...."

"I know," I broke in. interrupting for the first time—
"spring water with hemlock, aloes, opium, mandrake,
solanum, poppy-seed, asafœtida. and parsley-some or all of
the ingredients."

Poor Dorothy shuddered again at the recollection, as she
concluded bravely:

"And then it seemed that out of me half-darkness there rose a tall, pillar-like phantom: and, as it did so, I must have fainted. It is the last thing I remember until I found myself in Burgess's arms in the car. as though in a dream—a passing recollection—and then in bed with dear Ann nursing me. I have no knowledge of anything in between."

"Thank God." I said with great fervour: "and now you must lie back and rest. Try and forget those horrors; and, above all, don't talk to Ann or anyone else about them. Thank God we were in time to save you."

"And there is no trace of... of...?" she asked in an awestruck whisper.

"Of neither of them." I struck in quietly, to save her as much as I could; and under my breath I added once more, "Thank God."

So Burge and I left her, and went downstairs to his sanctum.

"I shall marry her, of course. Line," he said, "whatever may happen. She is not only pure in herself, but certainly untainted in blood or by any unconscious orgy; and it must be my joy and privilege in life to protect her from any all consequences of the evil wrought by others."

I gripped his hand.

"I know, old friend, and I first by God's grace to be able to exorcise this impregnated evil, if you will put your trust in me, and her—your most precious possession in the world—in my hands."

"Gladly will I leave it to you." said Burgess most heartily; "for, had it not been for your wonderful intuition and prompt action. I shudder to think what far worse things might have befallen my darling by now—and other innocent people."

And never in our long friendship have I felt so near or so close to the man I regard most in the world.

"I shall always feel," I said quickly, speaking with restraint, "to my dying day that it was given to me by a Higher Power to save not only the soul of Dorothy, but to wipe out this great and subtle danger to this country of yours which I have learnt to love so dearly from such long and close association."

It was getting too much like a melodrama in real life for my liking: so I went over to the sideboard.

"I'll shake you a cocktail, Burge," I said. "It won't do either of us any harm before lunch."

XVIII

And then it fell to my lot to work out the method and ritual of exorcism, and to make my preparations against the next full moon. which fell in the early hours of Wednesday, May 30. So I decided to anticipate its coming to fall by a few hours, and to act on the evening of Tuesday, May 29 between 8.32 and 9.16 when things were specially favourable to the exorcism of evil spirits and elemeutals. as that period was dominated by Mercury, the most bitter opponent of all such evil things—that is to say. Mercury was in 17°11 under the cusp of Seventh House, slightly to south of due west.

And so I laid my plans, while all went well at the house, both the invalids making rapid progress till we had grown more like a happy farmly party, with the other loyal actors in the recent drama coming to and fro, than a house with the shadow of great horror hanging over it, as we had been whilst awaiting the coming to fullness of the last moon.

Burgess was happier than any day could ever be long. and Dorothy was a different creature, though at times she grew restless, and a strange light would come into her eyes, as the moon approached fullness: but I made her sleep on the side of the house away from it. with blinds and curtains drawn close to keep its baleful light from her sensitive condition, both mental and physical- while each night I closed me windows of her room myself, and fastened them securely with my own hands, placing rye. garlic, and hyssop over every crevice. Our little Ann and her speedily recovering patient became inseparable under old Nature's wonderful system of mutual attraction: and. as we sat on the terrace with the garden ablaze with its bright armies of tulips in regiments and platoons, with their many-coloured "busbies" on their annual full-dress parade. I was the philosopher of the party, smoking my pipe contentedly and banking my hopes on the evening of the twenty-ninth.

I was all ready when it arrived; and Burgess and I, with Dorothy, left the house for an alleged drive in the dusk after an early dinner, at which the poor girl made but a poor pretence; and I could see marked signs of restlessness and both mental and physical stirrings within. And I don't mind confessing that I prayed as I have seldom prayed, as I sat at that dinner-table with laughter on my lips, a glass of wine in my hand, and a load of anxiety in rny heart.

Dorothy was dressed in the simplest white and only slipped on a light wrap, as it was a warm night; and she sat between us in the two-seater, supported morally as well as physically on both sides. I had explained everything to her, and she was glad to face the ordeal, though not unnaturally a little tearful and nervous; but, at her expressed desire, the ceremony was to be as private as possible.

It did not take us long before we reached the hatefulness of the Dower House hollow, a strange place in the dusk, and merely the empty shell of early associations; and I felt her tremble as we drove up the drive.

"Hold her tight, Burge," I said in a concentrated voice: "and pray as never before for your great love's sake."

And while I made my preparations swiftly, everything being arranged ready to hand, they knelt in the dusk under the old trees, which made it almost dark, the moon not yet being very bright or luminous.

First I drew a circle of seven-foot radius just in front of the old stone steps, all charred and scorched, and at the centre I made certain magical figures—in yellow chalk— representing Mercury: and round them I drew in white chalk a triangle within a circle of three-foot radius, having the same centre as the larger circle.

And then I took Dorothy and bound her securely hand and foot. and made her kneel within the inner circle, whilst round me outer circle I placed, at equal distances, seven hand-lamps burning olive oil. Then I built a rough altar of wood. about a foot to the south-east circumference of the inner circle: and opposite the altar, about a foot and a half to the far side of the circumference of the inner circle, I made a fire of wood, and placed over it a tripod with an iron pot, into which I poured two pints of pure spring water.

Then I added two drachms of sulphur, half an ounce of castoreum, six drachms of opium, three drachms of asafœitida, half an ounce of hypericum, three quarters of an ounce of ammonia, and half an ounce of camphor. And, when I had stirred and mixed it thoroughly, I added a portion of mandrake root, a live serpent, and a fungus.

Then. dipping a cup in the hot liquid. I dashed it over Dorothy, regardless of everything, and I poured the rest round her within the magic circle, calling, in a loud voice, three times upon the Evil Spirit—the unspeakable elemental who had defiled the temple of her body by taking up its dwelling therein—in the name Almighty God to begone.

And at that moment, with a strangled cry, Dorothy fell forward on her face, and a strange grey cloud, formless, yet not without form, seemed to pass upwards like a pyrarmd of foul smoke, disappearing and disintegrating into the air".

XIX

A week later Dorothy and Burgess were made man and wife at eight o'clock on a brilliant June morning, with the happy augury of the sun pouring into the old Saxon church on the fringe of the Clymping estate: and I had the great honour and happiness of standing beside them as "best man."

And this is the real end and true story of the appalling mysteries of the Brighton Road, still unrevealed so far as the public are concerned; and by now they have written them off in their short memories amongst the many undiscovered crimes chalked up against Scotland Yard, which is not always so much to blame as they think.

And now my task is finished, thank Heaven. This manuscript by the unanimous will of all concerned, is to be placed in the custody of the British Museum, and not to be available to the general public for a century—until all the actors in the ghoulish drama are dead and forgotten. Then the whole horrible truth can be revealed to those curious enough to dig up a tragedy a century old.

Postscriptum. I may be allowed to add that the future of Tony Bullingdon and Ann has in the meanwhile, solved itself upon lines I had foreseen for some time. Love, I often think, has a great deal to thank environment for; and certainly it is opportunity which makes the lover as well as the thief.

END

NOTE. Amongst the many works consulted and made use of by the author in studying the lore of lycanthropy, he wishes to make special acknowledgment of his indebtedness to Mr. Elliott O'Donnell's "Werewolves," the most comprehensive work upon the subject—in the English language, at any rate.

19597221R00111

Printed in Great Britain
by Amazon